Eight Is Enough

Books in the Holly's Heart series

Eight Is Enough

BEVERLY LEWIS

ZondervanPublishingHouse
Grand Rapids, Michigan

A Division of HarperCollinsPublishers

Eight Is Enough
Copyright © 1997 by Beverly Lewis

Requests for information should be addressed to:

ZondervanPublishingHouse
Grand Rapids, Michigan 49530

Library of Congress Cataloging-in-Publication Data

Lewis, Beverly, 1949–.
    Eight is enough / Beverly Lewis.
    p. cm.—(Holly's heart)
    Summary: Unable to understand why her mother and stepfather
want to have a baby when they already have six children, Holly
considers living with her father in California.
    ISBN: 0-310-20844-0 (pbk.)
    [1. Stepfamilies—fiction.] I. Title. II. Series: Lewis, Beverly, 1949–
Holly's heart series.
PZ7.L5846Ei 1997
[Fic]—dc20   96-43887
                                                CIP
                                                AC

All Scripture quotations, unless otherwise indicated, are taken from the
Holy Bible: New International Version®. NIV®. Copyright © 1973, 1978, 1984
by International Bible Society. Used by permission of Zondervan
Publishing House. All rights reserved.

Printed in the United States of America

97 98 99 00 01 02 03 04 /❖ DH/ 10 9 8 7 6 5 4 3 2 1

For
Holly's Heart fans
everywhere,
and especially—

Holly Allen
Holly Bradham
Holly Breuer
Holly Ferguson
Holly Holdren
Holly Loritts
Holly Pinkham
Holly Tang
Holly Weymouth
Hollie Zaborski

♥ Author's Note ♥

The idea for this book came from fans who thought Holly's mom should be expecting a baby and wondered how Holly would react to the news.

A big thank-you to my Kid Consultants—Julie, Amy, Janie, Brandy, Jon, Shanna, and Larissa. Mindie Verplank was so helpful with my questions about ultrasounds and high-school related things.

Andrea Worley got me thinking about middle names, specifically Holly's. So in this book you'll discover Holly's middle name for the first time. Thanks, Andrea!

Lori Walburg, my delightful editor, helps make the Holly's Heart series sparkle with her expert editorial touch, as always.

To fans who've sent cards, letters, and gifts, I want to say "God bless you, and thanks!" Your gestures of love bring joy and encouragement to this writer's heart. I never dreamed there were so many of you— loyal and exceptionally loving fans—out there!

Keep sweet, okay?

ONE

Not every girl finds out her mom's going to have a baby exactly one month before her fifteenth birthday. But that's what happened at my house.

During Sunday dinner, on January fourteenth, somewhere between meat loaf passing and potato mashing, my stepdad sprang the news on us. By us, I mean my ten-year-old birth sister, Carrie, and our four stepsiblings, who were also our blood cousins because their mother (our aunt) died and their dad, our Uncle Jack, married Mom.

Anyway, Stan, sixteen, Phil, eleven, Mark, nine, and the present baby of the family—Stephanie, just turned eight—and Carrie and I had totally different reactions to the bundle-from-heaven alert.

"This is so-o cool!" Carrie said. "If it's a baby girl,

I'm gonna start practicing my baby-sitting skills right away."

Mark crossed his eyes. "It better not be a girl. We've got enough girls around here!"

"Three girls and three boys," Carrie reminded him. "We're even-steven."

Stephie sat next to Carrie, pouting, probably not entirely because of Mark's comment. After all, she did hold the "baby spot" in our blended family, and by her frown I figured she wasn't ready to relinquish it anytime soon.

"If it's a boy," Phil said, "I'll be teaching him to figure square roots long before he can walk."

Uncle Jack leaned his head back and laughed. "Who knows," he said. "Maybe we *will* have another genius in the house."

Stan didn't say much. Neither did I. As far as I was concerned, this baby news was bad news. The house was already crammed to capacity with six kids. Absolutely no room for another body around here, pint-sized or not!

Mom's eyes shone as she laced her fingers through Uncle Jack's right there on top of the table. Pete's sake, they were acting like newlyweds. After all, it had already been over a year since they'd said "I do" and the Meredith-Patterson merger had begun. Four kids of his, two of hers, and soon there'd be one more—of theirs. What were they trying to do—show up the Brady Bunch?

Fork in hand, I poked at my green beans. Why would Mom want to start over with a baby at her age? Weren't there already zillions of chores to keep her busy, including the never-ending mountain of laundry?

Six kids plus two adults were plenty. Sometimes, too many. *Eight is enough*, I thought.

Besides, I needed space and plenty of time to write. Next thing, Mom would have me tied down baby-sitting after school. My writing project, a half-finished novella, would definitely suffer. And where would that put my writing career?

I sighed, bolstering myself with the thought that I still had some time to get used to the idea. Life would remain the same for a good while longer. After all, babies took nine months to hatch. I sighed, determined to grab every available minute between now and that not-so-blessed event.

Carrie pushed her plate back and leaned up in her chair, looking at Mom. "When's the baby due?"

Uncle Jack regarded Mom, who must've taken his stare to mean she should do the talking. "Our new little one"—and here she gazed into Uncle Jack's eyes—"is due on April twenty-fifth."

"April?" I blurted. "That soon?"

Carrie glared at me. I ignored her, trying to grasp Mom's statement, all the while doing a quick mental calculation. "That means you must be about six months along."

Uncle Jack nodded, eyes bright. He leaned over and kissed Mom's cheek. "We've already started picking out names." He began listing combinations of first and middle names for all of us to hear and approve or disapprove of.

I kept my head down, staring at my plate, trying hard to block out the sound of his voice, and the two of them in general, lovebirds that they were. It was plain to see how delighted they were. But what about the rest of us? Wasn't this a family matter? They should've called a family meeting—to vote on it. Our opinion counted for something, didn't it?

I felt numb.

"Holly-Heart," Mom said, her eyes penetrating me. "Everything okay?"

I shrugged. "I guess." No sense causing a scene. I'd have to work this out for myself. Still, I wondered why they'd waited so long to announce the surprising news.

Mom had appeared normal all these months. Oh, sure, she'd gained a few pounds and worn those loose flowing tops over her jeans, but that was her more casual style. Surely, she hadn't tried to hide her condition. Had she?

While we ate dessert, I thought back over the past months, searching for clues in my mind. Then it hit me. Memories of frozen dinners and occasional order-out pizzas. Unexplained doctor visits ... Oh yes, and there was the night I'd made spaghetti because Mom was too tired to cook.

Now I remembered. Back in October, when I was getting those bizarre mystery letters, Mom camped out in her room. A lot. Every day she had seemed exhausted. I had wondered if she might have the flu.

And Christmas? By then, things seemed perfectly fine. Mom had resumed her normal routine around the house, decorating for the holidays and sending out zillions of cards and notes. We'd had dinner guests off and on throughout December. People like Uncle Jack's coworkers and employees from his consulting firm. There were relaxed evenings spent caroling with church friends, but all during that time Mom had never said anything about a baby.

Until now.

Shocking as it was, my almost middle-aged mother was going to have another child. I should've been happy, but as much as I loved her, I couldn't muster up a speck of excitement.

The truth was, I wished she had confided in me. The way she always did when she was a single mom ... before Uncle Jack moved to Dressel Hills and married her.

On second thought, though, even sharing a secret like that with Mom wouldn't have made much difference. Not this kind of news. Bottom line: I didn't want another brother. Or sister.

Not now, not ever.

TWO

It was a gray Monday when I woke up. No sunshine—not a single mountain peak could be seen from my window seat where I peered out into the fog. A thick, dismal haze had enveloped our Colorado ski village.

I was gray, too. Inside.

During breakfast while Mom exhibited her sunny cheerfulness, my somber mood persisted. The grayness lingered with me all day, and by the end of seventh hour—swim class—I was exhausted.

While I dried off, my friend, Andie Martinez, buzzed over to me. "You're not yourself today. You sick?"

I forced a smile. "I'm okay."

Andie followed me to my P.E. locker. "C'mon, Holly-Heart, something's bugging you!" She grabbed my arm and held on. "I know you!"

With my free hand, I reached for my clothes. "Thanks for your concern, but I don't want to talk about it."

"Hey, whoa—I'm your best friend, remember?"

Nodding, I turned to look at her, wondering if I dared share my ridiculous family secret.

"What's wrong?" Her dark eyes reflected intense interest. "What is it?"

I shook my head, thinking how absurd it would sound if I told her. "Don't ask," I muttered. It was probably the worst possible thing I could've said. From past experiences, I knew that a few curt words never discouraged someone as persistent as Andie. Not dying-to-know-every-ounce-of-your-life Andie. Nope. My comment would simply egg her on.

"Aw," she pleaded, "just give one little hint."

I snapped my jeans. "It's not worth discussing, really."

She cocked her head. "Well, it certainly must be worth brooding over." She exhaled loudly. "Your chin's been dragging the floor all day."

I chuckled at her comment. Andie was like that. She'd pull out all the stops, say whatever she had to, to get me to succumb to her pleading.

"I'll be fine." I turned toward the mirror, brush in hand.

Andie followed close behind. "I can't believe you'd shut out your lifelong best friend like this, Holly Meredith."

I brushed through my hair, wondering how long

before she'd bug me to death and I'd finally tell her that my mom was pregnant.

Andie was so desperate to crack my secret, she even solicited help from another friend of ours, Amy-Liz Thompson, who'd just stepped out of the shower. "Hey, Amy!" she called to her. "Come help me talk sense to this girl."

Amy-Liz shivered in her towel, blue eyes wide. "Why, what's going on?"

"Look at her," Andie said to Amy-Liz, pointing at me. "Is this the face of a happy, well-adjusted freshman?"

"Spare me," I groaned. Her theatrical outbursts were too much.

Amy-Liz began to giggle. "Holly looks fine to me."

"But check out her eyes," Andie said. "Don't you see the disappointment, the pain, the—"

I intervened. "Go ahead and dry off," I instructed Amy-Liz. "I'm sure Andie'll get over this. Sooner or later."

Andie faked heart trouble, holding her hands on her chest. "Holly, you can't do this to me. I'm here for you, girl. It's you and me ..." She paused to breathe. "No, seriously, we need to talk. I know you're not okay, I can feel it!"

"I think you better get dressed," I told her. "Unless, of course, you wanna walk home."

Andie checked her watch. "Oh, no, the bus! I'll miss the bus," she moaned. "Why didn't you say something?"

"If you hurry, you can make it." I sat down, doing the loyal, best-friend thing—waiting for her.

On the way home, the bus stopped in front of the Explore Bookstore on Aspen Street, which was the main street in our tiny town. While passengers exited and new ones boarded, I stared at the window of my favorite bookstore. It looked like ... yep, it sure was!

"Hey, Andie! Is that what I think it is?" I strained to see the large poster displayed in the bookstore window. "Isn't that the new Marty Leigh book cover? It sure looks like her latest mystery novel. *Tricia's Secret Journey*. Hmm, it must be coming out soon." I squinted to see the date on the ad. "Wow, it's next weekend—fabulous! It'll hit the stores this Saturday."

"That's nice," she mumbled.

I turned to look at her. "What's wrong with you?"

"I'm not wild about mysteries," she replied. "You should know that."

"Well, I can't wait to get my hands on it." I looked back at the store window as the bus pulled away. "Marty Leigh's books are fabulous. I mean, you actually feel like you're there—in the book— living the story with the characters!"

Andie made a low, disinterested grunt. "Give me romance novels any day, anytime. Historical, fantasy, contemporary—doesn't matter, just so it's pure romance."

I slumped down, leaning my head back against

the rail behind the seat, thinking. "In the romance novels you read, how old do you like the main characters to be?"

She thought for a second. "Old enough to fall in love, why?"

"Just wondered." I was thinking about the marital romance going on between my mom and Uncle Jack. Sure, they were old enough to be in love and married and all—but way too old to be starting a new family.

"Excuse me, Holly. You're doing it again," Andie said.

"Doing what?"

"Spacing out." Andie touched my hand. "I'm here for you," she said softly. "Whatever it is, whatever is bothering you—trust me, I can help."

The bus turned right, heading for Downhill Court, my street. A light snow had begun to fall. The flakes swirled and floated down, their silvery whiteness turning to gray in the fast-approaching dusk. Cars in driveways looked gray as we passed. Yards and houses. Sidewalks, too. Everything was gray. Everything.

Trust me, I can help. Andie's words echoed in my mind.

But could she? After all, Andie's mom had given birth to twin boys three years ago when Andie was twelve. I suppose, if anyone could possibly understand how I felt, it would be my best friend.

Suddenly, she stood up, and I noticed the bus

was heading toward my stop. "I'm getting off here with you. Like it or not."

I didn't argue. If she wanted to come over, fine. I just hoped Mom would be resting. Or out running errands.

Anything to keep Andie from discovering the truth.

The two of us crossed the residential street one block away from my house, and as we walked, I decided I would usher her up to my room as soon as we got into the house. Because, knowing Carrie, she'd start talking baby stuff right under Andie's nose.

I was not ready to discuss the baby thing. I had to be cautious and do what I had to, to avoid it.

THREE

With my free hand on the doorknob, I poked my head inside the front door, wary of any activity that might call attention to the family secret.

"What are you doing?" Andie asked, nudging me forward. "You're not grounded, are you? Is that what's bugging you?"

While she babbled behind me on the porch, I scanned the living room. Vacant.

Good.

Inching myself past the door, I glanced at the dining room. Coast clear.

I breathed a sigh of relief. "C'mon in."

Andie looked at me cockeyed as I took her jacket and hung it in the hall closet. From where I stood, I could see Carrie, Stephie, Phil, and Mark standing with their backs to us out in the kitchen. They were leaning forward, all of them, studying something on the island/bar. I could only guess what they were looking at so intently. Probably baby furniture.

Not wanting to investigate, I steered Andie upstairs. "C'mon, let's go to my room." She cast a quizzical look my way, and we scampered up the stairs.

My bedroom was the second room on the left, the first being the bathroom. Carrie and Stephie shared the room straight off from the landing, and true to form, one of their CDs was blaring. Instantly, I wondered if having a baby in the house might—at least for the first few months—quiet things down a bit. Only a serious writer would think of such a thing, I guess.

Andie and I hurried into my room and closed the door. Goofey, my cat, was sunning himself on my window seat. One lazy eyelid lifted nonchalantly, then closed. I chuckled at his passive approach to hellos. "That was Goofey's welcome to you, in case you didn't know," I told Andie.

She snorted, not amused. "For some reason, cats hate me. I don't know why, they just do."

"Aw," I defended her. "That's not true. Goofey doesn't hate you. He knows you ... after all these years. Nah, he's just being a big, fat cat, minding his own business. Aren't you, baby?"

With that remark, Goofey raised his round, furry head and began to lick his paw, completely ignoring us.

"Better watch who you call fat," Andie said,

laughing as we flung ourselves on my canopy bed. I pushed my shoes off and got comfortable.

"Goofey's used to the truth about his size, aren't you, boy?" I leaned my head around the bedpost, sneaking a peek at him.

Andie watched me, and I could tell she was trying to be discreet in her scrutiny. "Holly?"

"Uh-huh?"

"Why don't you tell me the truth?"

I leaned up on my elbow. "About what?"

"You've been acting really weird today."

I was silent. Should I tell her or not?

Goofey leaped down off the window seat and came across the room, sniffing our stocking feet. Then, up ... he jumped onto the bed, parading past us like he owned the place.

"Goofey!" I said. "For Pete's sake, can't you see we're talking?" I reached out and pulled his shaggy gray-and-brown body over next to me.

"I think your cat's trying to tell you something," Andie said.

"Yeah? Like what?"

"Like to tell the truth ... spill your soul out to your best friend. Cats—er, animals—sense things like that."

Man, was she grasping at straws. I stroked Goofey's fur, contemplating my life. "It's just that things are way out of control these days," I found myself saying. "I feel like I'm about to drown in a sea of people."

Andie's eyebrows arched. "Huh?"

"It's not like I don't want to tell you about it, it's just . . ." I paused. "I don't know if I can make anyone understand what I'm feeling." I covered my face with my hands. "I'm so ashamed . . . I really should be happy . . . I—"

"Holly, don't worry about all that. None of those shoulds are important," she assured me. "The important thing is that you have someone to talk to. Someone to confide in."

"I know." I leaned back on the bed. "You're a very good friend, and I'm thankful we have each other—especially at times like this." I was actually going to tell her; I was that close. But someone knocked on my door.

"Coming!" I got up to see who was there.

It was Mom, wearing a brand-new maternity outfit. Her rounded stomach showed quite well. I kept the door from opening too wide. "What do you think?" she asked, twirling halfway around. "It's my coming-out dress."

"It's, uh, nice." I closed the door quickly.

"Holly?" she called. "There's more. I want to show you the slacks—you can trade off the skirt for a more casual look."

Andie got off the bed, looking bewildered. "Why'd you close the door on your mom?"

I wagged my pointer finger close to my mouth.

"Holly-Heart? What's going on?" Mom asked through the door.

"Uh, it's nothing," I replied, feeling ridiculous

about carrying on a conversation this way. "Can you show me later, I'm ... uh, sorta busy now."

There was an awkward pause. Even through the closed door, I could tell her feelings were hurt. Finally she said, "Well, honey, when you have a minute ... okay?"

I held my breath. What would she say next?

"That'll work," I said quickly, hoping she'd head down the hall to the master bedroom. Maybe put on her old jeans and one of those loose, flowing tops. An encounter with my pregnant mother was not the way I'd envisioned sharing the news with Andie. Not even close!

Leaning my head against the door, I listened for Mom's footsteps. When I heard the familiar crack of her ankle, I knew she was on her way.

I stood there, in the middle of my room, looking at Andie, wondering what she thought of all this. Of course, I didn't have to wait long to find out.

"I don't get it," she scolded. "Sounds like your mom's got a new outfit and you won't even look at it. What's the matter with you, girl?"

"I'm sure it seemed disrespectful, but there's so much more to it than meets the eye," I tried to explain.

Andie scrunched up her face. "I have no idea what you're talking about." She sat back down on the bed. "Why don't you spell it all out for me, starting with what you were saying right before your mom knocked on the door."

"Why? What was I saying?"

"It's not what you said, but what you were about to say." Andie was so good at this. Knowing when I was close to caving in with desired info. That's what happens when you grow up best friends.

I didn't blame her for wanting to know. Shoot, I'd kept my mouth shut long enough. I pulled on my hair, which was no longer waist-length. I'd had it cut to mid-back and spiral permed before the beginning of high school last September. Taking a deep breath, I turned to Andie. "I know this'll shock you, and believe me, I'm still in shock, but maybe you can help me."

Andie's eyes were saucers. "What ... what on earth are you saying?"

I sighed, mustering up the strength to tell my secret. "My mom's expecting a baby."

There. I'd said it.

The words were out. They were floating around my bedroom even now as Andie stared at me.

FOUR

Andie's head lurched forward. "You're kidding. Your mom's pregnant?"

"Even as we speak."

"Oh, Holly." She let herself fall back on my bed, making the canopy tremble a bit. "I thought you were going to say something horrendous."

"And this isn't?"

Andie sat up abruptly. "Get a grip, girl."

"But my mom's nearly forty and she's having another kid!" I insisted. "That's horrendous ... and scary."

Andie didn't buy it. "Healthy women can have babies way past forty these days." She studied me. "What's *really* bugging you?"

"I just told you."

"No, I mean, why is this such a hard thing for you?"

"I really thought you'd understand," I said, tears clouding my vision.

"Hey, look on the bright side, you might actually enjoy having a baby sister or brother in the house." She grinned. "I remember when Dad brought Mom home from the hospital with the twins. Oh, they were so-o tiny and cute."

She was putting me to shame. Still, I listened.

"Even now, in their sometimes rowdy three-year-old stage, Chris and Jon will come to my room dragging their teddy bears, and crawl up on my bed, pleading for a story."

"That's nice," I said softly. "But there's only five of you at your house."

"Five, eight, twenty," she said. "What's it matter, if you all love each other? Families are forever."

"Yeah ... forever and ever," I muttered.

"So snap out of it," she demanded. "I don't know what I'd do without my little brothers. I mean, if they hadn't been born—man, I'd be a lonely, only child!"

I could see that telling my secret to Andie had been a mistake. A big mistake. Not only did she not understand my feelings, she sounded like she was taking sides against me!

Suddenly, Andie got up and opened the bedroom door.

"What're you doing?" I asked.

She grinned. "I wanna congratulate your mom." And with that she started calling for her.

I hauled myself off the bed. Andie was showing me up significantly. The least I could do was go out and stand in the hall while she carried on her congratulatory remarks.

"Why, thank you, Andie," Mom was saying. "Maybe you and Holly can baby-sit sometime."

"Oh, I'd like that," she said. "I love babies." I tuned her out when she started saying how soft and sweet they were. I shouldn't have been surprised; after all, Andie had prided herself in telling everyone how she wanted a large family of her own someday. It was a fact of life with Andie Martinez.

❤ ❤ ❤

Much later, after supper dishes were put away and my homework was finished, I wrote in my journal.

Monday night, January 15th: It's not a happy sight. I mean, Mom parading around wearing bona fide maternity clothes. Now that I know she's expecting, she even looks pregnant!

I don't care what Andie says, it's not right for Mom and Uncle Jack to live in their own private world—planning secret things like babies and all—apart from the rest of the family. Don't they realize what bringing another child into the world is going to entail?

I stopped writing and thought of zillions of reasons why a family of our size (and parental age) shouldn't be added to. Had Uncle Jack and Mom counted the cost? Had they taken everything into consideration?

I picked up my pen and continued.

It's unfortunate that Andie and I don't see eye-to-eye. She's thrilled—literally. I can't believe how she carried on today with Mom, discussing the rewards of having a baby around. Shoot, I was embarrassed at the way she gushed!

When it comes right down to it, I think the thing that bothers me most is the timing. Mom and Uncle Jack waited till the last minute almost, to announce this. I mean, it would've been nice to have had seven or eight months to get used to such a monumental change. But, no. We weren't even given fair warning!

I bit on the end of my pen, wondering if on top of everything else, I'd have to give up my room to create a nursery. This room would be the logical place—just a few steps away from the master bedroom. But now wasn't the time to be thinking logic, was it? Logic had flown out the window back sometime in July, probably while I was out in California visiting my dad.

Resentment welled up in me as I thought of Uncle Jack and Mom discussing the possibility of having a baby together. Tears made two paths down my face, and I cried out to God. "It's not fair!" I prayed. "And I don't know what to do about it, Lord. Please, help me deal with this." I sobbed into my pillow. "I'm not doing a good job of it. I feel so deserted—by Mom, especially."

I stopped praying and lifted my head off the damp pillow. There it was. I'd just voiced it to God—the truth Andie was pleading for.

Rejection.

I felt left out. The way I'd felt after Daddy divorced Mom nearly seven years ago. That's what was bugging me, but I couldn't help what I was experiencing. Things like divorce left open wounds. About the time I thought my gash was scabbed over, beginning to heal, something like this was tearing it open—bringing all the insecurities back.

Later, after supper, Uncle Jack called a family meeting. My first thought was that it was a bit late to confer with everyone now. The baby was already on its way! Of course, it was a nasty, sarcastic thought, and I tried to suppress it.

The living room was draped with people. Stan sprawled out on the couch as usual; Phil and Mark sat near the coffee table counting strings of bubble gum. Carrie and Stephie had dragged their bean-bags down from their bedroom and were clumped together in the middle of the room, whispering. Mom sat in the rocking chair with hands folded on her stomach, emphasizing its roundness. Uncle Jack carried one of the straight-backed chairs in from the dining room and planted it next to her.

I chose the farthest corner of the room where a tall fica tree sheltered me as I sat cross-legged on the floor. Goofey purred in my lap as I stroked his thick fur.

"Tonight, let's begin with questions," Uncle Jack said. "Carrie and Stephie, in particular, have been curious about how babies grow inside a woman's body." He gave a fatherly glance at the girls sitting near his feet. "I think now is a good time to talk about all of that as a family."

I put my head down, staring at Goofey's adorable kitty ears and nose. *How ridiculous*, I thought. *Why is Uncle Jack doing the birds and bees thing? Doesn't he know we already know this stuff?*

Stephie's hand shot up. "When can we feel the baby kicking in Mommy's tummy?"

Mom spoke up. "The baby doesn't kick all the time. Sometimes she is asleep."

She? Mom thought the new baby was a girl!

Mark asked, "But if the baby's a boy, can Phil and I help name him?"

Uncle Jack chuckled. "We'll all help choose a name."

Now he includes us, I thought. *Now that it's too late ...*

Carrie twisted her long, blonde ponytail. "What if the baby turns out to be twins? What then?"

My stomach churned with the thought.

Mom laughed nervously at first. Then Uncle Jack spoke up. "The first ultrasound showed only one baby growing inside Mommy, but if there happen to be two, well, I'm sure we'll manage somehow. Won't we, honey?"

Mom nodded, a twinkle in her eye. She didn't seem opposed to the idea at all! I, however, was appalled. Surely, God—in his mercy and love—wouldn't let something like that happen.

After everyone else was finished asking questions, I managed to voice my greatest concern. "Where's the nursery going to be?"

Mom and Uncle Jack looked at each other. The way their eyes caught made me even more worried. They'd already discussed moving me out of my room, I was sure of it!

"We haven't completely decided all the details," Mom said, hesitantly. "For the first few weeks, the baby will sleep in a bassinet in our room."

Uncle Jack reached for Mom's hand. "We've thought of various options, including putting all three of you girls in our master bedroom and taking the room Carrie and Stephie have now for ours."

"Which would leave my room for the nursery?" I sputtered.

"That's just one possibility, Holly," Mom said softly. "We still have time to plan."

I wasn't totally ignorant. The option they'd just voiced was the most viable choice. For them.

I fumed as I thought about moving out of my room. Of being stuck in the same bedroom with two little sisters—and snooping ones, at that!

How could Mom do this to me?

FIVE

I spent most of my Tuesday morning in a daze—hardly remembered anything that happened in either government class or algebra. Choir was a blur, too, although I did remember working on our songs for All-State choir auditions, which were coming up in a few months.

The nursery scenario kept cropping up, though, pounding my brain like the rhythmic wail of a newborn baby. To think that Mom and Uncle Jack would actually tear me away from my fabulous room—the room Daddy had planned for me. It was unthinkable that Mom would allow Uncle Jack to voice such a thing.

The house at 207 Downhill Court housed my roots, my very life. A girl almost fifteen oughta have some say in where she lay her head at night—not to mention where she wrote her stories. And kept a written record of her life.

My future writing career might be completely thrown off course if I were uprooted and forced to be in the same room—master suite or not—with Carrie and Stephie. It was outright injustice.

During lunch, I poured out my heart to Andie. Even though she didn't think the overall baby thing was anything to lose sleep over, she was sympathetic to the pain of giving up my room for the new baby.

"My parents would never have done that to me, and we had *two* new babies at our house!" she said.

Paula and Kayla Miller, our twin girlfriends, had been listening. But when they spoke up, they weren't exactly on my side.

"Perhaps you're getting yourself worked up over nothing," Paula suggested.

Kayla nodded. "Once the baby comes, you might surprise yourself and be willing to share your room. Who knows?"

"I doubt it," I replied. "How would you like to go home to the sounds and smells of a newborn while you're trying to write a novel or figure out the latest mumbo-jumbo algebra problem?"

Paula's ears perked up. "Did I hear you correctly? Did you say you were writing a novel?"

I shrugged. "Well, it's not actually a full-blown one. It's more like a novella, you know, a mini-novel."

Andie whipped out her pocket dictionary and began to read. "A novella is a short novel."

"Okay, miss know-it-all." Reaching for the dictionary, I read it for myself. "Yeah, I guess Webster's right—that's what I'm writing."

Andie slipped the tiny dictionary into her shoulder bag. "Well, that's settled." She propped her elbow on the table, leaning over next to me. "So ... when do we get to read your masterpiece?"

"Maybe never."

"Never? C'mon, Holly, you know you need a second opinion," Andie said. "We're precisely the ones to give it."

Paula and Kayla were nodding their heads. "What could it hurt?" Kayla said. "We wouldn't think of being hard on you. We give our solemn promise."

Paula picked up her sandwich, inspecting it as she spoke. "Maybe the manuscript will turn out to be absolutely perfect and then, when we tell you so, you'll decide to dedicate your first published book to us."

"Hey, I like that," Andie chimed in. "Will you please dedicate a book to your best friends?"

I giggled. "You guys are too much."

"Well, if you won't let us read it, will you at least tell us the story line?" Paula asked.

Andie whispered, "Is it romance?"

Paula and Kayla leaned in, waiting for my response.

"Definitely, it's a romance. But I can't tell you anything more."

"Aw ... ," Andie groaned. "You can't keep us in the dark like this."

"Why not?" I said. "Are you worried that I'll be old and gray before I ever find a publisher? That you'll have to wait forever to read it?"

"No way," Paula said. "You're a good writer, Holly-Heart. I'm positive you'll find a publisher."

Kayla smiled. "Wanna know what I always read first when the school paper comes out?" Paula and Andie were nodding their heads in agreement. "It's the Dear Holly page. I simply adore the way you answer those letters."

"You're very clever," Paula said. "No publisher in his right mind would abandon the opportunity to work with such a talented young author."

"Girls, girls," I said, blushing. "Enough."

We ate in silence for a few moments, then Paula brought up the fact that Marty Leigh's next novel was coming out soon. "Did you see the poster in the window at Explore Bookstore?" she asked.

Andie answered for me. "Boy, did she ever. You should've seen Holly hanging out the window, drooling all over the side of the bus."

"Not quite," I laughed. "But I am counting the hours till Saturday."

"So are we," the Miller twins chorused in unison, which didn't happen often, but when it did, we always got a kick out of it.

"Speaking of authors," Paula said, "did I tell you about the cool letter I received from Marty Leigh?"

"You wrote her?" I was in shock.

Kayla grinned. "I wanted to, but Paula had more courage. So she wrote for both of us."

"I'll bring the letter tomorrow—actually, it's a newsletter highlighting the next books in her series, but she also sent a personal reply in her own handwriting!"

Now I was leaning forward. "You asked her questions?"

"My letter to her was almost like an interview by mail," Paula replied. "I couldn't believe it, she went through one by one and responded to every single question. It was astonishing."

"Wow, you're not kidding," I said. "Do you have any idea how many fan letters she must get every month?"

"Probably tons," Kayla said.

Andie was eating quietly, obviously not interested. Of course, if Marty Leigh's mysteries had included romance, she would've been hooked.

"Tell me some of the questions you asked her," I said, dying to know.

"Well, Kayla inquired about her favorite foods, hobbies, things like that, but I asked about clothes preferences, and how she got started writing."

I was all ears. "What did she say about that—how she got started?"

"Her grandfather was a journalist," Paula continued. "She's quite certain that she inherited his love for the printed word."

"Wow," I said. "When did she first get published?"

"I asked her that," Paula said. "She said she'd

had a short story published in a regional newspaper when she was only thirteen."

"Hey, just like Holly-Heart!" Andie piped up. "Remember that cute story you wrote?"

Of course I remembered. It was my very first byline. You never forget fabulous stuff like that.

"What was the title again?" Kayla asked.

"Love Times Two," I said. "About two girls liking the same guy."

"It was actually fiction based on the true story of Holly and me—and Jared Wilkins," Andie reminded them.

"Thank goodness those days are long gone," I said.

"Except that Jared's still in love with you," Paula blurted.

I shook my head. "Please, don't remind me."

Andie played with the gold chain at her neck. "How's Sean Hamilton these days? You two still writing?"

Andie hadn't asked about him for several weeks. I figured she had come to grips with my long-distance romance. At last.

"Oh, Sean's great," I said. "In fact, he's coming here to ski next month—maybe Valentine's week."

"Ewe-ee," Andie cheered. "Just in time for Holly's fifteenth birthday and her first real date."

"That's right," I said, grinning. "I'm saving my first date for Sean."

Andie was pretending to play a violin under her chin. "Aw, how sweet is true love," she sang.

I didn't comment. The girl had romancitis!

"Is he coming alone?" Paula inquired.

"He's bringing a group of kids from his church youth group—they call themselves 'Power House'—and the group's just for sixth through eighth graders. Anyway, Sean's one of the leaders."

"He sounds like a great guy," Kayla said.

"He is," Andie said, probably referring to last summer when she met Sean for the first time. "Hey, maybe our youth group should join them when they come. We could have a snow party!"

Paula smiled, displaying her perfect teeth. "Maybe we should let Holly decide about that."

Andie and Kayla stifled their laughter.

"Oh, c'mon," I said, "there'll be plenty of time for me to spend time with Sean." I gathered up the trash at our table.

"Uh-oh," Andie said, "sounds like they've got this romantic visit all planned."

I felt my cheeks blush. Sean and I had discussed and planned his trip here—in fact, we'd sent several letters' worth of plans back and forth. He was beginning to share more freely in his letters, about his feelings for me. I, on the other hand, was careful not to seem too eager. Sean, after all, was older. By two years.

I wanted God's perfect plan for me as far as the boy I dated—and most of all, the man I would ultimately marry.

Andie got up with her tray just as Stan, my brousin (cousin turned stepbrother), and two other guys walked past our table. Kayla glanced up, following Stan with her eyes. I wondered about it.

Two years ago when the Miller twins first moved to Dressel Hills, Kayla had confided in me about Stan. She'd had this major crush on him back in Pennsylvania, where the Millers had lived in close proximity to Uncle Jack's family, long before Aunt Marla passed away.

After the funeral, months later, Kayla's father encouraged his friend and prospective business partner, Uncle Jack, to move to Colorado for a fresh start. Kayla was thrilled to discover that Stan was attending the same school in Dressel Hills.

For the longest time, I thought she'd given up on Stan. But just now, the way her eyes lit up when he passed by, I had a feeling she wasn't exactly over him. I decided not to say anything, though. Kayla was supersensitive.

Quickly, the Miller twins and I gathered up our trays and carried them to the kitchen, where Andie was waiting.

"Have you told Sean Hamilton about your mom yet?" Andie asked.

"You mean about the baby?" I frowned. "Where in the world did that thought come from?"

Andie tapped the top of her dark, curly head. "I was just wondering. Sean seemed like a kid-crazy sort of guy when we were out in California, remember?"

She didn't have to remind me. Sean's married

brother had two kids. In fact, Sean wrote often about his niece and nephew.

"I'm sure I'll be telling him soon," I found myself saying, wishing Andie hadn't brought up the topic just as we were heading off for fifth hour. I'd had a tough enough time concentrating during my morning classes. I couldn't afford to space out during French. The new dialogues were getting harder and longer this semester, and our teacher, Mr. Irving, wasn't as lenient about prompting us these days.

Le bébé. French for: the baby. I would have to get used to the baby idea eventually. Maybe saying and writing the words in another language would help.

Then again . . . maybe not.

SIX

After school, I headed for the public library several blocks from the high school. I hadn't been able to focus on my writing since last Sunday when the baby news had been heralded at dinner. I was eager to get going on my project again.

Among the rows and rows of tall bookshelves and long study tables, I began to work on my novella. *Okay, fine*, I thought, getting serious about chapter eight of my book. Only four chapters to go. When the first semi-polished draft was finished, I would go back and fill in, delete, and tighten and refine. Who knows, maybe I'd get brave and try to find a publisher. Mrs. Ross, my English teacher, had mentioned certain publishers who only wanted works by young people. Maybe I could talk with her.

Unfortunately, I was going to have to deal with a

new baby brother or sister in the next few months, and that could possibly hinder me from completing the book. Maybe, if I was lucky, I'd finish the book by the time I was twentysomething. By then, though, those publishers searching for young authors wouldn't want to see my work. Nope. I'd be too old for them and probably not old enough for the other book publishers. *Sigh*.

I jumped right in where chapter seven left off. My main character, Julianna, had just received a letter from her boyfriend, Christopher. As I wrote the lines, I thought of Sean. In no way did I want this story to be about him and me, fictionalized or not. I scratched out what I'd written and started over.

Thirty minutes later, I stopped writing and was tempted to reread what I'd written. A mistake for me—deadly, actually—in terms of slowing me down and putting my mind in the editing mode. My creative side would get bogged down; I'd lose my flow. But my curiosity won out, and I went back and read each word, scrutinizing the whole.

None of it, however, sat well with me. I was a perfectionist when it came to writing. So, discouraged, and not looking forward to those inevitable baby discussions at home, I decided to stay right here and switch gears. I decided to write a letter to Sean, even though Mom would be wondering where I was. We had this after-school phone rule at our house. If any of us were going to be longer than one hour after school, Mom expected to be informed.

I'm not sure why I didn't get up right then and

use the pay phone. Call home. Something in me lashed out in defiance, I suppose. I ignored my better judgment and stayed put.

It was time Sean heard from me about the latest turn of events at the Meredith-Patterson residence. Actually, I wouldn't have been too surprised if he'd already heard the news. Sean attended the same church as Daddy, and Daddy's mother, my grandma Meredith, still kept in touch with Mom. No doubt, Mom had told my grandparents her news.

I took a clean piece of notebook paper out of my three-ring binder and began to write.

Tuesday, January 16
Dear Sean,

Hi! How're you doing? I've been wanting to write for a couple days. Bet you're having great weather there. It's cold and snowy here, but, hey, what can you expect this close to the Continental Divide?

My algebra grades are up now, but I still have to work hard at keeping them there. Sometimes I wonder how this kind of math is ever going to help me as a writer. That is, IF I ever get published again. Maybe I'll need to know algebra when it comes time for me to double-check my royalty statements someday. Ha!

Not long ago, I read about five well-known authors and how they worked. One said that getting published the first time was relatively easy, but the second and third time he really had to work at it. I can't help but wonder how I ever landed that first story with Marty Leigh's cool teen magazine.

Right now, if I didn't have the published story to prove it, I'd probably doubt it ever happened.

By the way, my favorite author's next mystery is due out this Saturday. I know you aren't interested in books for teen girls, but my friends, Kayla and Paula Miller, and I are going to be the first ones inside the bookstore when it opens! Andie said she's sleeping in—she could care less about mysteries.

I stopped writing, wondering how I should tell Sean about Mom's baby. There wasn't any creative way to say it, I decided, so I picked up my pen and flat out informed him.

I wouldn't be surprised if maybe Daddy's already heard this news, and so you might know about it, too. My mom's expecting a baby the end of April. It's not all that surprising really, and I should've guessed Mom would want more kids, but when reality hits you in the face, you have to be ready to pack up and move out of your bedroom. What I'm complaining about is just what I said. Most likely, I'll have to give up my private domain.

Can you believe it? How would you feel if this were happening to you? But then, there's only two of you in your family, and now, since your brother's much older and married with his own family, you probably feel like an only child. Right?

Writing this, I stopped and thought of Andie and the many times she'd remarked about what fun a big family would be. A lot she had to learn! Big families were okay, but when eight people tried to cram into a house built for four, even with the new addition, the result could be sheer frustration.

Mom and Uncle Jack, however, never seemed to notice how stressful life on Downhill Court had become. Is that what happened when people fell in love? They blocked out the negative parts of their life altogether?

I finished off the letter to Sean, trying very hard not to sound like a whiny, spoiled brat. Packing my schoolbag, I headed for the library doors.

❤   ❤   ❤

At home, Mom was sitting on the living-room couch trying her best to follow crocheting instructions for a yellow baby sweater and booties to match. Carrie and Stephie were helping her roll the bright-colored yarn into a smooth, round ball.

"You're late," Mom said as I flung my coat onto a hanger in the hall closet. "And you didn't call."

"Lost track of time."

"We have an understanding in this house, Holly-Heart." She looked at me with accusing eyes. "That rule has been a long-standing one. You know better."

"Sorry." I took off for the kitchen, not waiting for her response.

"Excuse me, young lady," I heard Mom say. She only used those kinds of words when she was upset. "I'm not finished with you."

I crept backward through the dining room and into the living room. Carrie was covering her mouth with her hand. Stephie, too, smirked, watching my every move.

"Pull up a chair," Mom said to me. "Let's talk."

"Not in front of them," I sneered, shooting darts at the would-be roommates of my not-so-distant future.

"Holly Suzanne Meredith!" barked Mom.

Quickly, I sat down in the rocker. "I'm sorry," I said, thinking now was a good time to say it.

"If you don't follow rules, you know there is always a consequence."

I nodded. "I'll try to do better next time."

Carrie opened her mouth. "If there is a next time!"

Mom shushed my sister, and turned to me. "This is seriously important business."

"Well, I think it's time we cancel out some of those little kid rules," I pled my cause. "I'm a freshman now."

"Rules help families run more smoothly," she said, obviously not eager to lay down her defense. "I'm willing to compromise, perhaps, but not do away with the rule completely. Letting me know your whereabouts after school hours is still essential, even during your high school years."

"Can't we talk about it, at least?"

"Your stepdad will be home for supper; we can discuss it then." End of discussion, she'd evidently decided, and she went back to her precious crochet needles and baby project.

"I'd rather not talk about this in front of the whole tribe," I spouted.

Mom's head shot up. "Tribe? Since when do you

47

refer to your family as a tribe? Holly, what's gotten into you?"

"I learned it in government class," I said glibly. "A tribe is more than one family with common characteristics and interests, although in our case I'm not so sure." With that, I got up and walked out of the room.

I could still hear Mom calling for me to *come right here—right now, young lady* as I slammed my bedroom door.

SEVEN

Slamming doors and spewing annoying words always got me in hot water. And I mean hot. Uncle Jack didn't take too kindly to one of us sassing his bride of fourteen months. Mom, who was known to take occasional outbursts in her stride, had come down on me harder than ever.

Shoot, if I hadn't done some mighty fast talking—as in sincerely apologizing—I would've been grounded from now to Valentine's Day. Of course, I was smart enough to admit that I was wrong; Mom was right. Still, I chafed at their correction—their unified front.

"Your mother says you want to modify the calling rule," Uncle Jack said as we settled into the downstairs family room for the intimate meeting. The rest of the family had been shooed away—

upstairs. Mom and Uncle Jack sat on the sectional, halfway across the room from me. I observed them from the bottom step, where I'd chosen to sit, keeping a safe distance.

I got the ball rolling. "After school, I think I should be allowed to have two hours of freedom. To go to the library or do whatever. That would be perfect," I said, hoping I sounded polite enough to wage a victory.

Mom spoke up. "It's the 'do whatever' that has me concerned." She sighed. "How do I know you won't go hanging around the mall?"

"What's so wrong with that?"

"Holly," Uncle Jack reprimanded me. "Watch your attitude."

"But all my friends are allowed to do whatever they want after school. For as long as they want."

"All your friends?" Mom asked.

"Well, you know," I said. "I was just trying to make a point. Sorry."

Uncle Jack frowned suddenly. "No, I don't believe you are sorry, and until you can discuss things respectfully, your mother and I won't be interested in any sort of compromise."

Rats, I blew it. I pulled myself up off the step. Sitting and being lectured to—no fun. Things around here sure weren't anything close to the old days, before Uncle Jack came along.

To be honest, I was sick of the superprivate world he and Mom had created for themselves. Honeymooners? Lovebirds? Who cared! Their plans no longer seemed to include me. Maybe I was jealous; maybe that was it. Anyway, I seethed all the way up to my bedroom.

❤   ❤   ❤

On Wednesday, Paula brought her letter from Marty Leigh to school. I went wild with excitement, and Paula let me make a copy of it during lunch. Reading and rereading the letter was the high point of my entire week.

Unfortunately, the days flew by without another opportunity to talk about the after-school phoning rule with either Mom or Uncle Jack. Maybe it was just as well. Mom's head was somewhere in a blue or pink cloud called babyland, and Uncle Jack was just as preoccupied with his work.

First thing Saturday, I met Paula and Kayla at the bookstore on Aspen Street. Bright anticipation shone from their eyes. "Holly, hi!" they called to me. The girls were dressed in their typical weekend attire of blue jeans and warm sweaters. Their bright pink-and-gray ski jackets were new, Christmas presents probably.

"Looks like there's no line," I said, glad to see them.

"I can't believe we're the only Marty Leigh fans in town," Paula said.

"All the better, my dears," I chanted. "We want to be sure to get some pre-signed copies, right?" I peeked in the frosty window. "Hey, look! There's a brand-new floor display loaded with books—it must've just arrived."

"I know, I came by yesterday after school," Paula said, "and the display was nowhere in sight."

I shivered with excitement and from the cold. "This is going to be so cool." Glancing at my watch, I knew we wouldn't have to wait much longer to actually hold the books in our hands.

"I wish Marty Leigh would make more public appearances," I said.

"Big-name authors usually only hit the big cities, don't they?" Paula suggested.

I laughed. "Dressel Hills doesn't exactly qualify for city status, but she was here once a couple years ago."

A familiar face greeted us with an enthusiastic smile as the store manager unlocked the doors. "Good morning, young ladies," he said. "I have a feeling you might be interested in my latest shipment. Am I correct?"

"Never more so," Paula said, as we scooted inside and dashed to the Young Adult section.

Kayla was first to find a book with the author's autograph. "Here's one with Marty's full name and a special greeting."

Paula and I crowded her. "Oh, I hope there's more," I said, snatching up several from the display and finding the title page. "Fabulous! At least three books are signed."

We stood there scrutinizing the cover and then flipped to the back and read the summary. Each of us held the treasured new books in our hands at last.

The book was about a girl named Tricia who'd decided she wanted to get to know her estranged father better and had initiated a joint custody petition to the courts.

"This isn't a mystery," I said. "At least, it doesn't seem like one."

"Keep reading," Kayla said.

"Why doesn't Ms. Leigh come out with two or three books at a time?" Paula lamented. "Do you have any idea how fast I read these? Honestly, I cannot put them down!"

"Personally, I devour them," Kayla said. "They're addictive, but in a good sort of way."

I nodded. "I can only hope to write like her someday, with page-turning suspense and chapter cliff-hangers to die for!"

The twins exchanged secretive glances, grinning at each other. Paula reassured me that if I continued writing I might offer Ms. Leigh some great competition someday.

Someday, I thought as I waited at the cash register.

Someday, if there weren't a screaming half sister or brother to anticipate, who'd eventually grow into toddlerhood with even louder noises and, heaven forbid, into a school-age snooper like Carrie and Stephie.

Someday might never come. Unless . . .

I reread the summary on the back of the book, my mind spinning nearly out of control. It said right here that Tricia Joellyn Engle, the main character, needed space—a break from her mother and sisters. Why else would she go through all the trouble of pleading to live with her dad part of the year? Did Tricia really want to get to know her dad better? Or did she just need some breathing room?

Joint custody, I thought. *Hmm, is this an option for me?*

Daydreaming, I thought of the warm beach sand, the pounding waves, the natural, peaceful setting of Daddy's beach house in southern California. What better option could an aspiring young author have as a place to live and work?

The store manager's voice broke into my thoughts. "Will that be cash today?"

"Oh, sorry." I dug into my wallet. "Here you are. And thanks!"

"Thank you," he replied.

Kayla and Paula suggested we hit The World's Best Donut Shop before heading home. "But I'm dying to go home and read," I said, hugging my book.

"You have all weekend for that," Paula said, taking my arm and nudging me forward down the snowy sidewalk. "Besides, we have a surprise for you."

"A surprise?" I went willingly, of course. Curiosity ruled my life. "Aren't you going to give me a hint?" We were within sniffing distance of the pastry shop.

"No hints," Kayla said. "Just put on your best smile."

"Uh-oh. This isn't about a guy, is it?"

Paula blocked my view into the shop. "Come along," she teased. "You won't regret it."

"I better not." Sean Hamilton came to my mind, and I wished he might be sitting in a booth waiting for me.

Now *that* would be a fabulous surprise!

EIGHT

But it wasn't Sean. It was Jared.

"What's *he* doing here?" I whispered as we opened the door to the pastry shop.

Kayla said it first. "Act happy."

"Yes, please look as though you're thrilled to see him," Paula whispered, then led the way.

We made our way across the room to a table set against a window. Window boxes filled with fake red geraniums framed the sill inside. I couldn't imagine why Paula and Kayla thought coming here and finding this guy waiting was such a good surprise. But I did as they advised and smiled.

"Hi, Jared." I slid into the booth across from him.

"Holly-Heart! Glad you came," he said as Kayla and Paula divided up and sat on opposite sides of the table—Paula next to Jared.

Why was he here waiting for me? I wondered.

There was no flirting involved—surprise, surprise. Jared pulled no punches either; he got right to the subject at hand, although I had no idea that what he had to say would turn out to be so incredibly fascinating.

"Have I ever told you about my uncle in Chicago?" he asked.

I shook my head. "I . . . I don't think so. Why?"

He ran a hand through his thick, brown hair. "My uncle just acquired a small press—a publishing company—and believe it or not, he's looking for quality writing from young authors. And I mean young, like around our age."

"You're kidding!" I sat up instantly.

Jared's eyes lit up. "Andie says you're working on a short story or something."

"Word gets around," I muttered.

"Well, my uncle's the publisher like I said, and he's putting together an anthology—compiling short stories hopefully by lots of different teenage authors."

I took a deep breath. *Can this be happening?*

"Holly, are you okay?" he said.

"I'm fine, it's just so . . . so . . . ." I reached for the pastry list at the edge of the table beside the wall and began to fan myself. "It's just that I can hardly believe it. Are you sure about all this?"

Jared reached into his jeans pocket and pulled out a letter from his uncle. He handed it to me. "Here, read it for yourself." I could feel his gaze on me as I read silently. "I'm planning to submit a story—well, it's a little longer than a short story," he said. "Are *you* interested?"

Kayla and Paula smiled encouragingly, waiting for my reply.

I folded the letter. "Are you kidding? I've been living for this moment all my life. To be published in a book, a real book!"

Jared glanced at Paula. "Thanks for getting Holly to come." His grin made his blue eyes twinkle.

I poked Kayla. "So you guys set this up with Jared? You knew about it?"

"Aren't you glad?" she said.

"This is the best surprise I've had in years!" I opened my wallet. "Who wants a donut? I'm buying."

Jared resisted my offer, but I managed to pull it off anyway. Kayla and Paula were nearly clucking with delight, even opened their bookstore bags and showed Jared the new Marty Leigh book.

"Be careful, don't get any chocolate on it!" Paula warned.

Jared listened as the three of us chattered about how wonderful Ms. Leigh's writing was. "She can't be any better than some of the male authors I've read," he countered.

"But if you've never read a Marty Leigh mystery, how could you possibly know?" I interjected. "She grabs you in the first paragraph. Here, let me give you an example."

I wiped my sticky fingers, then licked the worst

ones in anticipation of holding the new book. "Oh, rats, wait here, I'll be right back." Quickly, I headed for the ladies' room, where I washed the stickiness off my hands.

When I got back, Paula and Kayla were informing Jared in no uncertain terms that Marty Leigh was the contemporary queen of teen novels. "There's no one better, trust me," Kayla said. "And I've read tons of books."

"Well, if she's so great, let's hear some of this wonderful writing," Jared said, baiting me as I sat down. "Are your hands clean enough to touch the golden pages?"

I slapped the book at him, playfully. "Okay, now you judge for yourself." I began to read. Out of the corner of my eye, I could see Jared leaning forward, listening. After three paragraphs, I stopped.

"Whoa, don't quit now," he said, playacting. "Keep going, I think . . . I feel it . . . it's happening . . . oh, no, I'm being sucked into the story!"

Paula punched his arm. "Act your age."

"No, duh," I said, closing the book and studying Jared. "I suspect what is lacking here is a mature female mentality. Obviously."

Jared groaned. "It's not that I don't think the author is good, she is, but . . . I just tend to think that men have a better grasp of the English language."

"Oh, puh-leeze," I said.

We finished our donuts as we continued to talk.

"I'll let you know where to send your manuscript," Jared said before we left.

"The entire manuscript?" I asked. "Your uncle wants the whole thing?"

"Don't worry, mine's not finished yet either."

I slung my purse over my shoulder. "So how long do I have?"

"The cutoff date is April something. I'll have to check and let you know."

"April's perfect," I said, thinking that if I hurried I'd have plenty of time to write and rewrite my novella before the Meredith-Patterson offspring arrived.

"April's the birth month for Holly's baby brother or sister," Paula commented as we walked outside together.

"Yeah, Stan told me," Jared said. "Big surprise, huh?"

I wrinkled my nose. "Whoopee-doo."

"You don't approve?" he probed.

"At their age it seems very weird."

The city bus was heading toward us. "Sounds like you're not too thrilled about it," he said.

"No double duh."

Paula took my side. "Think how you'd feel having to move out of your room to make space for a nursery?"

"Really? You'll have to do that?" Jared asked.

"Let's put it this way, it's been discussed as an option," I said. "But I have a few options of my own."

"Like what?" Kayla asked.

"I have to think them through first," I replied, rather secretively, although I hadn't intended to encourage curiosity on their part.

"Hey, don't get some wild idea about moving away to California or somewhere," Jared said, almost desperately. "Your friends need you here."

His words thoroughly shocked me. Not the friends part, but what he'd said about California. How could he have possibly known what I was thinking?

I stared at him, this gorgeous hunk of guyhood. Jared Wilkins had been my first love, or crush, or whatever it was I'd suffered through back in my seventh-grade days. Anyway, here he was, connecting with me somehow. Almost pleading with me to stay.

The brakes screeched as the lumbering bus came to a crunching stop in the snow. We scurried down the sidewalk in the frosty air and boarded the bus. All of us.

Jared scooted in beside me behind the Miller twins. For a split second, the thought that they had set this up—this seating arrangement, shoot, this bus ride home—crossed my mind. Had they?

"You're not really thinking of going to live with your dad, are you?" Jared asked softly.

I felt brave suddenly, so I tested the waters. "Why not? He's my real father."

"That's true, but what about the rest of your family?"

"Mom has Uncle Jack, if that's what you mean."

Jared was silent, hands stuffed into his jacket pockets.

"There isn't room in that house for me anymore." I surprised myself by blurting out. Kayla and Paula turned around, aghast.

Paula spoke up. "That can't be true, Holly. Remember your uncle had that addition built onto the back of the house over a year ago?"

"It only added two more bedrooms, and those are filled up with brousins—Stan, Phil, and Mark. There's no way Mom will put a newborn, even if it's a boy, that far away from her at night."

"Maybe when the kid's older," Jared mentioned. "Stan probably wouldn't mind sharing his room with a little brother. I wouldn't."

"You?" I was shocked. "You're not into little kids, are you?"

"Hey, what's the big deal? Kids are kids."

It was a male thing to say. Truth was, guys had no idea what they were talking about when it came to babies—or toddlers, for that matter. Sean was the exception, however.

He knew exactly what it took to make a little kid happy. I'd seen him in action, and I was convinced he'd be a good father someday. No way could Stan or Jared ever begin to match that kind of behavior.

"Hang in there, Holly," Jared said as the bus turned toward my street. "No need to freak out and do something impulsive that you might regret."

"How do you know I'd regret moving to California?"

Again, the twins turned around wearing stunned expressions. "Relax," I said to them. "Jared's the one freaking out."

"Guess again," Paula said.

"All right," I admitted. "But don't you dare breathe a word of this to anyone. Not even Andie. I have some phone calls to make before I decide anything."

I felt Jared's body slump down in the seat next to me. He was hurt. Actually hurt at the thought of my leaving.

I stood up, ready to exit the bus, but Jared wouldn't budge. "Don't do anything today, Holly. In fact, why don't you wait a few days before you call your dad?" He'd done it again. He'd said out loud what I was possibly planning.

"Jared, for Pete's sake, will you move your legs?" I stood there waiting for him, blocked in my seat.

Reluctantly, he slid out of the seat, standing up to allow me to pass. "I'll call you later, and don't say not to."

"We'll call you, too," the twins said together.

I smiled at the unison comment. "Bye!"

"Thanks for the donuts," called Paula.

"Yeah, thanks, Holly-soon-to-be-author," shouted Kayla just before the door closed behind me.

I should've felt good as I crossed the street and began the brisk walk home. Only one block to go with thick flakes of snow falling faster and faster.

With the new Marty Leigh mystery snug in my purse, the sweet taste of donut on my tongue, and the prospect of being published, I attempted to cheer myself.

Surely, a phone call to California would make me feel better. Hearing Daddy's voice always did that. So did staying at his big, luxurious beach house.

My plan for joint custody was absolutely perfect.

NINE

I waited till after lunch to call Daddy. Mom and Uncle Jack had gone downstairs to look at a department store catalog of baby furniture. All the kids were outside playing in the snow, even Stan.

Going to the kitchen, I picked up the portable phone and carried it to the living room. Quickly, I pressed the numbers, remembering to include the area code.

Busy signal.

Rats, I thought. Just when I'd found a tranquil moment on my end, Daddy or Saundra, his wife, was on the phone.

I waited a few minutes, then tried again. Still busy. Frustrated, I got up to return the phone to the kitchen.

Crash-crinkle-smash! The front picture window

broke, sending glass flying through the air. The snowball shot through the dining room and landed near the kitchen island yards away.

Uncle Jack appeared in a flash. "What was that?"

"Someone broke the window," I said, thinking that if I hadn't tried to get through to California the second time, I might've been hit by the snowball or cut by the shattered glass.

By now, Stan and the boys were on the front deck inspecting the damage. Carrie and Stephie crept up the front walk, looking worried.

"Man, you're in for it now," Mark said, poking Phil.

"I didn't mean to hit the window," Phil said, quickly apologizing.

"No one ever does," little Stephie chimed in, her eyes big as saucers.

Uncle Jack took the incident in stride, not losing his cool. He was like that—calm and collected in the face of problems. "We'll have to get a replacement for the window," he said, instructing Phil to run inside and get a dustpan and broom.

"What about a heavy blanket with some duct tape?" Stan suggested. "Wouldn't that help block out the cold?"

Mom appeared at the door, holding the baby catalog. "A blanket wouldn't be secure enough," she said. "Not nowadays."

I figured she meant that it wouldn't be safe. Someone—a burglar or whatever—could easily pull a blanket down and come in the house while we were sleeping. Rob us blind.

Uncle Jack was a sensible man. After all, he had a wife with a baby on the way, not to mention six kids. He would protect us and make the house secure for the night.

"We'll head downtown right now and see what can be done," Uncle Jack said. "Stan, run and find my measuring tape in the tool cabinet."

Stan scurried off to the garage. Phil returned with the broom and began sweeping the shards of glass off the redwood deck.

"Be very careful," Mom warned, as Phil swept. "I don't want any of you ending up in the emergency room."

Carrie pulled Stephie back, away from the glassy mess. "C'mon, let's finish making our snowman," she said.

"We weren't the ones throwing snowballs," Stephie assured Mom, over her shoulder.

Mom smiled and nodded her head. "Go have fun."

Stan returned with the retractable measuring tape, helping Uncle Jack with the measurements.

Mom's expression showed concern as I shivered, watching. "Why don't you come in and get warm, Holly?" she said.

I didn't want to be inside with her alone—didn't trust myself. I might say something I'd regret later.

"I'll be okay," I said, not surprised when she left

for a moment and came back holding my coat and a knit ski hat.

"Here, put these on." She handed them out the door.

I had no choice but to obey. Uncle Jack wouldn't stand for open rebellion at this juncture. Besides, he had his hands full at the moment.

Turning, I looked out over the front lawn, which was covered with several inches of powdery snow. Stephie was patting the head on the snowman, packing the snow down. Colorado snow didn't have much moisture content, and most of the time, we used buckets filled with water to make our snowballs and snowmen. Wet snows usually came in the early spring. Those were the best for snow forts and snowmen.

"Come help us," Carrie called to me.

"Okay, just a minute." I ran inside to get some waterproof mittens. The phone rang while I was rummaging around in the hall closet, searching. "I'll get it," I called to Mom, who was still surveying the scene of the accident.

Hurrying to the kitchen phone, I picked it up. "Hello?"

"Holly-Heart, it's good to hear your voice." It was Daddy. "How's my number-one girl?"

"Hi," I said, pleased to hear from him. "I tried to call you earlier." I leaned around the corner of the kitchen, checking to see if Mom could hear my end of the conversation.

"Oh, really?" he said. "That's interesting; I believe

we may have been trying to call you around the same time."

"How's Saundra?" I asked. "And Tyler?" Tyler was my stepbrother, Saundra's son.

"Fine, fine, everyone's doing well here. And you? How's Carrie?"

I chuckled. "She's outside making a snowman."

"Sounds like she's having fun. With her stepsister, no doubt."

"Yeah." I felt funny about springing the custody thing on him now, within earshot of Mom. This wasn't the time.

"So . . . were you calling about something in particular?" he asked.

"Well, I really want to talk to you about something."

There was awkward silence between us. Then he spoke. "You don't feel free to talk?"

"Not really."

"I understand," he said. "Well, when it's convenient, why don't you call me collect? You have my office number, don't you?"

"It's in my wallet."

"Well, I'll be in and out of the office tomorrow, so keep trying if you don't get me right away."

"I will."

I thought he was about to hang up when he said, "Sean Hamilton's brother mentioned something interesting to me yesterday at work." I knew Sean's older brother worked with Daddy. In fact, he'd been one of the ones who'd first talked to Daddy about becoming a Christian.

"I think I know what you're going to say." I crept toward the dining room to check on Mom's whereabouts. It seemed she'd gone upstairs. Maybe to lie down.

"Your mother's going to have another child." He said it frankly, almost without feeling, as though it were just another financial fact or sales projection.

"Yeah, in April. And that's kind of why I wanted to talk to you." I'd found my opportunity. Mom was safely upstairs; Uncle Jack was outside with the rest of the family. "Do you think I could come out there for a while?"

"Now? During the school year?"

"Well, maybe not right away, but soon?"

He paused for a moment. "Are you asking if you can come here to live, Holly-Heart?"

"I . . . I guess I am." It was strange, now that the words were out, I wasn't so sure. "For part of the year, at least."

"Is everything okay there, I mean, are you happy?"

"Well, no, not really."

"Is this something your mother and I need to discuss?"

I wasn't going to get Mom involved. "No, I don't think that's necessary. Besides, she's busy planning for the baby. I wouldn't want to upset her."

"I see." He sighed. "Is this idea partly because of the new baby? Is that why you want to come out?"

"It got me thinking, I guess you could say."

"You're unhappy with your mother then? Are the two of you not getting along?"

Now it was my turn to exhale. "Oh, we don't fight about anything, if that's what you mean, we just don't ... we don't really ever talk the way we used to. And ... and she kept her pregnancy a secret from me all this time." In some ways, I felt better sharing this with him, but in another way, I felt like I was betraying my family here.

"A secret, you say?"

"That's how it seems." No way was I going to complain about the cozy marriage Mom had settled into with Uncle Jack. There was no reason to mention my feelings about any of that. Daddy was a Christian now, and he and Saundra were doing okay, too. The old days of fantasizing about Daddy and Mom getting back together were over. Besides, the fantasy was just that—a fantasy.

"Well, I'm wondering if things won't change for you once the new baby arrives. You're one big happy family now."

Yeah, right, I thought. *Guess he's not wild about me moving out there.*

"I wish you'd let me come," I said softly, feeling hurt.

"Let you? I'd love to have you. Don't you know that, Holly? But things like this aren't decided in an instant of anger, or whatever it is you're feeling, dear. Why don't you think about it ... pray about it, too, and we'll talk later."

He's putting me off.

"I won't change my mind," I vowed.

"Please do pray about it," he said.

"I'll tell Carrie you said hi."

"Please do," he said. "Good-bye now."

Usually, I would say 'I love you,' but the words didn't feel natural today. Not one bit.

I hung up, heavyhearted. Daddy had seemed hesitant on the phone. He hadn't responded the way I thought he would. I was more than disappointed. Shoot, it threw a wrench into all my plans.

I'd have to find another way to convince him.

Soon.

TEN

All day Saturday, I kept my conversation with Jared about his publisher uncle a secret from Mom and Uncle Jack. In many ways, I wanted to savor the information—keep it to myself. Not out of revenge. Well, maybe it was.

I purposely showered and did my hair early in the evening so I'd have uninterrupted time to read my new book.

Tricia's Secret Journey had grabbed me on the first page and wouldn't let me go. Even when Kayla called, I could hardly pull myself away from it.

"Hi, Kayla. What's up?"

"Well, you know, Paula and I told you we'd be calling."

"Right."

"So what's going on with you, anyway? Are you really thinking of moving to California?"

"Nothing's certain, if that's what you mean."

"Oh, Holly, we don't want to go through this moving thing again with you." She was referring to last year when Uncle Jack had announced he was moving us to Denver. Those were depressing days for all of us.

"I won't put you through anything traumatic," I replied. "If I do get my dad to consent to it, I'll be rejoicing. You should too."

"You've talked to your dad already?" She sounded frantic.

"A few hours ago."

"And? What's he think about it?"

I sighed. "I'd rather not say."

"Didn't it go too well then? Is that what you're saying?"

"Look, Kayla, I really shouldn't be discussing this with anyone right now. Do you understand?"

"Sure, but don't worry about us spreading it around," she said. "You have our word of honor."

"Thanks." I was dying to get back to my book.

"Oh, Holly, something else. This has nothing to do with you and your dad. I was just wondering if you know ... well, that is, I thought you might have an idea if ..." She stopped.

"What's wrong, Kayla? What do you wanna know?"

"I'm sorry, it's just so hard. I hope your stepbrother isn't anywhere nearby. Is he?"

I glanced around, even leaned over the stair railing and looked down. "Nope. All clear."

"Okay, here goes," she said. "Do you know if Stan has a girlfriend?"

"Stan?" I giggled. "I was right. You are still crazy about him."

"Oh, Holly, please, please, don't breathe a word of this to anyone. Especially not—"

"You don't have to worry about that," I reassured her. "As for girlfriends, Andie was his last, and, as you know, that's been over since last summer."

"Oh, good. I'm so relieved."

"Relax, Kayla. You don't have anything to worry about. Stan's only human, honest."

"Well, I better get going. My mom wants to use the phone."

"Okay, well, tell Paula hi for me," I offered.

"I will. See you at church tomorrow."

"Yep. Bye."

Bingo! Kayla wanted Stan to ask her out. Now, instead of dying to get back to my book, I was thinking of ways to "help" my brousin get the message. Without telling him in so many words, of course. Kayla would have my neck. I'd have to be discreet.

Once my thoughts about getting Kayla and Stan together faded, I curled up in bed with my book. I found myself absolutely absorbed with the character, Tricia Joellyn. She was so much like me, had most of the same problems in life, and more than anything wanted to get away from her present family and live with her dad for a while. The amazing thing was, Tricia's dad wasn't all that enthusiastic about her joint custody idea either. Just like Daddy. In fact, the reason why Tricia called an attorney after the initial talk with her dad was the very reason I'd secretly considered making a phone call to the law firm where my mom had worked as a paralegal before she remarried.

My reason? I felt rejected, and I wanted my father to know I was serious about this. Getting an attorney involved didn't have to mean I was hostile. I certainly hoped Mom or Uncle Jack wouldn't see it that way.

Monday, I would make the call from a pay phone during lunch. No one would ever have to know.

ELEVEN

Jared came right in and sat down beside me in Sunday school the next day. Like he owned me or something. Danny Myers sure didn't like it. At least, that's how it looked from where I sat, catching his annoyed expression.

Actually, Danny seemed rather forsaken these days, without a girlfriend—namely, Kayla. Being the studious sophomore that he was, I figured he didn't care much about the boy-girl thing anymore. Evidently, I was wrong.

"You hanging in there?" Jared whispered in my ear.

"Why shouldn't I be?"

"I'm talking about the California situation."

I looked him square in the eyes. "I know what you're talking about, Jared."

He must've gotten the message that I didn't want to discuss it. Not here, in front of everyone. Abruptly, he changed the subject. "How's your story coming?"

"Haven't written another word."

He looked surprised. "You *are* interested, aren't you?"

"You know I am, it's just ... well, everything's happening at once."

Our Sunday school teacher came in. Jared said no more about either matter. Still, I felt strange sitting next to him like this, knowing that Sean would be coming to see me—we'd be having our first real date—in three and a half weeks!

❤   ❤   ❤

On Monday, Paula and Kayla surrounded me at my locker first thing. They were worried about my custody plans. Both of them.

"It's not like I'm divorcing my mom or anything!" I explained.

"Who's not divorcing who?" It was Andie.

Stunned, I turned around. The twins were silent, too.

"Well, excu-use me, I can tell when I've stumbled into unwanted territory!" She spun away on her heels.

"Andie! Come back!" I called to her.

She did. In a flash. "What's going on?"

Of course, I had to tell her. There was no way around it. I couldn't shut out my very best friend forever. So as quickly as I could, I summarized the state I was in, leaving out the secret phone call I'd planned to make during lunch.

"This is craziness," Andie yelped. "I can't believe you'd go to such measures—to get attention, no less."

"You're wrong," I snapped. "That's not what this is about."

"Could've fooled me." She rolled her eyes at the twins, who were doing everything they could to support my decision by staying calm.

"Holly's going through some rough waters right now," Paula said, putting her arm around my shoulders.

Andie laughed. "Hey, welcome to life."

"She's in need of encouragement," Kayla piped up, "not . . . not—"

"Not what I have to say?" Andie asked. "Is that what you're trying to tell me?"

"Calm down." I grabbed her arm the way she always did to me. "Your opinion counts, honest. Please don't freak out about this. If everything goes as planned, I'll be back here in time for the last half of summer."

"Huh?" Andie said. "You actually wanna leave in the middle of the school year?"

"It's really very complicated," I said. "Besides, I don't think any of you really understand what's going on with me. Read my lips, there's eight people living under one roof at my house. Does that mean anything to you guys?"

The twins stared at me, blinking their long eye-lashes.

Andie sighed. "Like I said before, what's the big deal?"

"It's crowded at my house, and I can't think. I'm losing my privacy just when I have a chance to be a book author."

"A what?" Andie hadn't heard. "When did this happen?"

"Saturday at the donut shop. Jared was there. Paula and Kayla set it all up." I filled her in quickly. "And by the way," I said, remembering how the twins had seemingly concocted Jared's showing up just as we were going to get donuts. "I think we should talk about last Saturday ... the bus ride home and all."

"The what?" Paula asked.

"Don't play dumb with me," I said. "I know what you're trying to do. He asked you to arrange things, right?"

"Are we talking Jared Wilkins here?" Andie butted in.

"None other," I answered.

Paula and Kayla remained stone silent.

"C'mon, girls, I have a strong feeling about this," I said, staring them down.

"So does Jared—about you," Paula spoke up.

"Not this again." I remembered that Paula thought I should talk to Jared about who was writing me those mystery letters last fall. She'd actually believed he knew something. Of course, he did in the end, but Paula had encouraged me to have lunch with him about it.

Funny. Paula herself had been interested in Jared when they'd first moved here from Pennsylvania. Maybe she still was ...

"Listen, if you think Jared's so wonderful, why don't you go out with him?" I suggested. "Me? I've got myself the best guy in the world."

On that note, the four of us disbanded. The bell had rung for homerooms.

❤   ❤   ❤

At lunch, I was able to sneak out of school, grab a burger at a fast-food place nearby, and find an available pay phone all in less than fifty minutes.

"Hello, I'm calling to get some preliminary information," I said. *Was this what I really wanted to say? Preliminary information?*

I always got nervous when I had to talk to professionals. Especially strangers.

"One moment, please," the receptionist said.

A paralegal came on the line. She identified herself. Instantly, I recognized her as one of Mom's friends at the firm. "How may I help you?" she asked.

She'd know me in an instant, I thought. Pete's sake, she was in my mom's wedding to Uncle Jack! I almost froze, almost hung up.

I was counting on her not recognizing my voice. "Well, I'd rather not identify myself if that's okay. I'm simply gathering information at the present time."

"I'll help you as best I can," came the professional-sounding voice.

I took a deep breath. "I'm wondering how to go about arranging for a joint custody situation between myself and my divorced parents."

"Are you of age?" the woman asked.

"I'll be fifteen in twenty-three days."

"Then I believe you would have some say in what happens to you."

"What do you mean, what happens to me?"

"I'm talking about in abuse situations a foster home is often called upon. The Department of Social Services—"

"No, no, I'm not saying any of that. I've never been abused in any way." I stopped to catch my breath. "All I want to know is—how difficult would it be to get my parents to change custody arrangements against their will?"

I could just imagine her face. She probably wondered what rock I'd crawled out from under.

"Excuse me, miss, I don't believe I understand. Are you telling me neither of your parents is in agreement with joint custody?"

"I'm not completely sure about my mom, but I don't think my dad's very interested."

"So your mother has full custody of you at the present time?"

"Yes."

"Then that's a tricky one," she replied. "I think you'd better make an appointment with one of the attorneys. And, about the fees—"

"I have enough money saved up for the first visit," I said. "If it's not too expensive."

"Well, I think maybe we might be able to arrange a court-appointed attorney for you. But that would require a court hearing. Would you like someone here to set that up?"

This court talk scared me silly. I honestly didn't know anymore. "Uh . . . I'll have to think about it," I said. "I can call you back tomorrow. Is that all right?"

"Of course."

"Thank you."

"You're very welcome," came the reply.

I returned the phone receiver to its cradle and opened the folding doors to the phone booth. The winter wind blew hard against me as I walked up the hill toward the high school. I wondered how I'd have the nerve to pull things off.

But I had to try. There was no giving up. I would call Daddy again.

Tonight.

TWELVE

"Do you mind if I use the phone?" I asked Mom before supper. She was peeling a sinkful of potatoes with Carrie's and Phil's help.

"Long-distance?" Her eyes gave her away. She knew.

I nodded.

"Your father?"

"Yes." I could feel the tension between us.

"Now's as good a time as any," she said. "Why don't you use the phone upstairs ... in our bedroom?"

"Can I talk to him, too?" Carrie pleaded to Mom as I hurried out of the kitchen, through the dining room, and up the stairs.

I closed the door to the master suite, feeling my

heart pound with anticipation. "Daddy?" I said, when he answered.

"Well, hello again. How are you?"

Formal, unnecessary greetings, I thought. *Let's get on with it.*

"I don't know for sure what to do next," I said. "I called a law firm today. Talked to a paralegal."

"You did *what?*"

"I just wanted to get some information," I said. "Nobody here knows I called."

"Holly, dear, what are you doing to yourself?" He sounded upset. "I thought we agreed you were going to think about this—take some time before deciding anything—and talk to the Lord about your feelings."

This sounded strange coming from Daddy. All those years before, he never cared about what God thought about anything. He lived his life the way he chose to. Left Mom, Carrie, and me for the big city. Big-time job. All that.

But now. Now he'd come to a place of faith in Christ. Now he talked to God regularly. Like I did. Or like I used to, I should say. Lately, God and I weren't on speaking terms much at all.

"Holly?" he said gently. "Can we talk about this?"

The lump in my throat was growing. "I don't want to stay here anymore," I said, tears spilling down my cheeks. "They're taking my room away ... they don't care how I feel about ..."

I couldn't go on. The ache in my throat pinched my words.

"You don't think they care how you feel about the baby?" Daddy prompted me. "Is that what you're trying to say?"

I squeaked something.

"If you lived with your mother part of the year and with me the other months, how would this affect your education? Have you thought about that? And what about your sister? What would Carrie think?"

"Carrie doesn't think," I protested. "She's starting to act like . . . oh, I don't know what's happening to her."

"Now, don't be hard on your sister. You know what she's going through," he said. "You remember what the preteen years were like, don't you?"

"Yeah, but there's no way I'm staying here just because of her."

My statement didn't seem to shock him. "What about your mother? How would such a change affect her?"

"We've already discussed her. She's in love with Uncle Jack, with her new baby. Her life is perfect."

Daddy made no comment about that. "But your friends. Wouldn't you miss Andie? And all the others?"

"Sure, I'd miss them, but it wouldn't be like I was going away forever. I'd come back for half the year and then come live with you the rest of the time. A simple rotation—it's easy."

He sighed. I actually heard him sigh! Like this was a burden or something. "How did the attorney's office advise you?"

"Listen, Daddy, if you're not in favor of this," I blubbered, "then I need to know right now. Yes or no."

"Well, I must say that I certainly don't approve of your reasoning for joint custody. If you ask me, I think you're being a bit selfish."

"*I'm* selfish? Mom's selfish! She's the one destroying my life. She's the one getting everything she wants."

"Hold on, honey. I think you're overreacting, and I suggest you put your mother on the phone."

He was ordering me around! My father was ruining everything—complicating my already horribly messed-up life!

"Mom's busy," I said. "She can't talk now."

"Well, then, I'll have to give her a call later," he said. "I wish you weren't so upset. Good-bye, Holly."

That was the end of that. Daddy had practically hung up on me!

Putting the phone back on the nightstand, I hurried around the bed toward the door. On my way out, I noticed more skeins of yarn piled up on the chair in the corner.

Greens, yellows, and a pearly white. Mom was playing it safe, crocheting colors that would work for either a boy or a girl.

I stood there daydreaming. Scarcely could I

remember the day Carrie was born. I was four years old when Mom and Daddy brought her home from the hospital. Hard as I tried, though, I couldn't remember ever holding her as an infant. Oh, sure there were tons of pictures, and sometimes from studying scrapbooks I got the mistaken impression that I actually remembered the occasion or how the person looked. But it was really only the pictures tricking me, making me think I really remembered.

I shook off the images from the past and headed to my room, frantic. Daddy was going to call Mom and blow the whistle on me. How could he? If he loved me at all, he'd go along with my idea.

Stephie was across the hall playing the same miserable CD she loved over and over. Without saying a word, I tiptoed up to her room and closed her door.

"Hey!" she hollered. The door flew open. "What do you think you're doing?"

"I have to write something," I said, towering over her.

"Well, I'm not stopping you."

"No, but your music is," I scolded. "So either turn it off or shut your door." I made a move toward her, and she misread me and started yelling for Mom.

I grabbed her by the shoulders. "Stop it right now, Stephie. Mom's busy."

Truth was, I didn't want to recite any part of my

phone call to her. In fact, I wished I'd never called Daddy in the first place!

"I'm telling," Stephie yelled, and for an instant, I saw parts of myself in her. The way I'd been acting for the past week or so. Ever since the baby news.

"Fine," I said. "Go ahead, yell and scream. Act like a spoiled brat, see if I care."

That shut her up. She turned around and flounced back to her bedroom and slammed the door.

Relieved, I raced to my room and closed my own door.

I knew I had about forty-five minutes before supper. Forty-five precious minutes! I needed to make tracks, there was no getting around it. If I didn't hurry and finish this story, I'd lose my golden opportunity, as Daddy used to say.

Picking up my pen, I began to write.

Five words later, I was twirling the pen. Stuck.

What would I do if Daddy refused me? I'd be on thin ice. And all the while, Mom was planning for her new baby while Uncle Jack's buttons were bursting.

I tried to push myself, force myself to write more, but it was no use. Moods were a problem with me. Either I was revved up, ready to write, or I wasn't. Today it wasn't coming. Not at all.

Maybe today's writer's block was a good thing, because the phone rang and when I answered it, Jared was saying, "Hi, Holly-Heart. Are you okay?" Like he cared or something.

I would've positively died if Mom had announced that Jared was on the phone, calling to me for everyone in the house to hear.

"I'm fine, thanks. How are you?" I asked.

"You don't have to be so polite with me," he was saying.

This was weird. Was Paula right? Did Jared still care? I couldn't imagine in my wildest dreams going back to him. Not now, not ever.

"Why are you calling?" I asked.

"Can't a friend check up on another friend?"

"I guess I don't understand."

He didn't answer.

"C'mon, Jared, you don't have to play games with me. Why'd you really call?"

He cleared his throat. Was he nervous? "I can't forget you, Holly-Heart. I just can't."

"That's what you say to all the girls," I retorted. "I know you, Jared."

"You do know me. That's why I can talk to you. That's why I'm telling you if you push this custody change, I'll never speak to you again."

I snickered. "Hey, that wouldn't be so bad."

"Give a guy a break." I knew I'd hurt him. But he'd hurt me. Bad. Last year. And then again last fall at the start of school. He and Amy-Liz Thompson ... seeing them together. *That* hurt.

"I'm really sorry about this, Jared. But I don't think there's any hope for us. Ever."

"You sound so sure."

"I am. But thanks for calling. And if I do end up

going to live with my dad, I hope you won't clam up on me. You won't, will you?"

A long pause.

"Jared?"

"I can't believe you'd wanna leave us all behind, Holly-Heart. Doesn't Dressel Hills mean anything to you anymore?"

He'd hit my soft spot. I loved this ski town. My roots were here. Always and forever. Still, it didn't hurt to branch out—see the world. That's what Andie kept saying all last summer.

"I would miss Dressel Hills," I managed to say. "You know how I feel about my friends here. And you, too, Jared. We've been friends since seventh grade. Nothing can change our past. But the future ... the future's coming up fast. I don't want to deal with what's happening here."

"I think maybe you've hit the nail on the head," he said.

"Huh?"

"You know what I think, Holly? You're running away from your problems. Why don't you ask the Lord to help you handle things?" He paused for a moment, then said, "I've been doing that a lot lately. It really helps."

"I know it does." But I hadn't prayed for over a week.

"Well, I'd better go. Don't be mad at me for calling. Promise?"

I smiled. "I'm not mad. We're friends, right? Good-bye, Jared."

"Not good-bye, Holly-Heart," he said softly into the phone. "How about—see ya later? That's much better."

My heart sank as I hung up the phone. What was Jared Wilkins doing to me? Again.

THIRTEEN

Five after six.

I read the glowing numbers on the bedside digital clock. I'd awakened before the alarm.

Tuesday morning—another day of school. Lazily, I swung my legs out over the bed and sat there, rubbing my eyes.

Yawning, I tried not to think about my conversation with Daddy. He hadn't called back to talk to Mom. Thank goodness. On the other hand, anticipating his call to her would slowly drive me crazy—eventually. I could only hope that he'd had a change of heart and wasn't going to get Mom involved from his end. Man, that would be so awkward. Thorny, in fact.

I went to my window seat and knelt down to pray. "Dear Lord," I began. "It seems like a long time since I've talked to you about what's going on in my life. I know you've helped me many times before and I'm very thankful.

"Lately, it seems everyone's been recommending that I come to you with my hopes for joint custody. So here I am, wishing I could say some positive things about my life, but unfortunately I can't. Not right now, at least.

"Things are worse than crazy. I've got this baby brother or sister coming along soon. But you know all about that. Anyway, I need help with it. Sometimes I feel so hostile toward this kid who's not even born yet. I resent Mom and Uncle Jack, too, for not including me—not sharing the fact with me early on, when they first found out. Things aren't the way they used to be with Mom and me. We used to be so close. Unbelievably close."

Goofey nuzzled against me. I held him gently while I finished my prayer. "I wish this idea I have about living with Daddy half the year wouldn't be such a big deal to him—or to Mom when I tell her about it. Why can't things be more simple, the way I view them? I don't want to hurt anyone; I just need a break."

I stopped praying. Someone was tapping on my door.

"Come in," I said, still kneeling.

"Morning, Holly." Mom studied me with eyes of love. "I'm sorry to disturb you. You were praying, weren't you?"

"Just started."

"We could talk later if you like." She moved back toward the door, as though she were going to exit.

"Uh, that's okay."

Mom tied the loop on her terry cloth bathrobe loosely. Feeling uneasy, I motioned for her to sit on my bed. She went and sat down, then patted the spot beside her.

"I don't want to cause additional problems between us," she began, glancing down as though hesitant to speak. "Things have been awfully tense lately. Honestly, I don't know where to begin."

I sat next to her, watching her face. *What's she trying to say?*

Without warning, Mom's eyes were bright with tears. "This is one of the hardest things I've had to encounter in a long time."

"What is it, Mom? Are you okay?"

"Someone said ... well, I must confess that I heard this straight from a friend. You're thinking of going to live with your father ... you've contacted an attorney's office."

I thought of the paralegal I'd spoken to on the phone. "I should've known she'd recognize my voice," I muttered.

Mom's eyes held a strange hurt, almost a disbelief. "Such a thoughtless thing to do, Holly. I'm surprised at you—inquiring about joint custody like that!"

I steeled myself. "Lots of kids with split families go back and forth between their divorced parents."

"That's never something I would've agreed to."

"Maybe not back then when you and Daddy split

up, but now ... now I'm almost fifteen. I should be able to decide certain things. It ... it, uh, might help us, you and me, if I lived with Daddy for a while."

"I wish you would've talked to me about it first." She reached for my hand. "It's because of the baby, isn't it? You're angry with me."

I glimpsed over at Goofey, who was curled into a tight ball on my window seat. "Bottom line, I hate the thought of losing my own space—this room. Stan has a huge room all to himself. So should I."

Mom listened.

I continued. "Daddy built this house for us—you, Carrie, and me. He designed the house with his kids in mind. How could I ever begin to let you take my room and turn it into a ..." I sputtered angrily at the thought. "Into a nursery for your baby?"

She responded softly, almost sadly. "Holly, do you really think we're scheming to take away your room? It's only one of the options we have in mind."

"I need time to write." I ignored what she'd just said. "I have an incredible opportunity to become a published book author. This year! But I need my space, and I have to be able to think and write with-out—"

"Why didn't you tell us?" she interrupted. "When did you find out? How ... what's it all about?"

I told her everything. The initial conversation with Jared. All of it.

Mom literally beamed. "What good news! Oh, I'm so excited for you."

"Can you understand better now?" I said, using the writing project as an excuse for being upset. Of course, it wasn't entirely true.

"I wish you had told us immediately," she said, "when you first heard about the publisher."

And I wish you'd told me about the baby when you first found out, I thought, biting my tongue. That was the number-one reason I was so ticked.

She let go of my hand. "I really wish you hadn't gone behind our backs and called the law offices."

"It might seem like I went behind your backs, but I didn't, not entirely," I admitted. "I've talked to Daddy about it—last night when I called him."

She gasped. "You mentioned this to your father?"

"He'll let me come live there. I'm sure of it," I answered with confidence. "I'll have a large, private bedroom suite and study area. It's perfect, don't you see? Besides, Daddy can have his attorney look into it. No hassles for you and Uncle Jack."

Mom's face fell. "I'm not an unfit mother, Holly," she whispered. "No court in the land would change custody based on a whim."

I was fired up. "They would if I took the stand and testified. Not against you or Uncle Jack, but just to say where I wanted to live. How I feel about it. Judges are leaning more and more in favor of the child these days." I sighed. "What is in the best interest of Holly Suzanne Meredith? Have you thought of it that way?"

"For heaven's sake, you sound like a spoiled . . ."

"Go ahead, say it. I'm a spoiled brat."

"Where are you getting such ridiculous, selfish ideas?"

I didn't dare tell her I'd stayed up late, reading *Tricia's Secret Journey*. Most of my ideas had come from Marty Leigh's shrewd and conniving characters. None of them Christians.

"Where on earth?" she demanded.

Mom had just lashed out at me. Now I had to turn the tables on her. Stick up for what I believed in. "Why shouldn't living with my father part of the time be an option for me? Why?"

She shook her head. "Please, Holly. Don't push this."

"But what if adding another kid to this household destroys my entire future as a writer?" I insisted. "What about that?"

She eased off the bed slowly. "You're not making sense."

"I know the feeling," I mumbled under my breath. "By the way, when can we discuss the phone-calling rule?"

"Maybe we won't need to." There was a strange, icy edge to her words. "If you're moving out, why would you need to call home after school?" With that, she burst into tears and left the room.

I could hear Uncle Jack's gentle voice at the end of the hall as she went to him for comfort, no doubt.

Whew, was I in trouble now!

FOURTEEN

I kept running into Jared Wilkins all day at school. Although I felt responsible for breaking Mom's heart, I felt confident enough in myself to remind Jared that we were no longer going out. Repeatedly.

I told my friends about Jared during lunch. "When will he ever get it through his head? He and I . . . we're through."

Andie, Paula, and Kayla listened, sympathizing with me.

"You know Jared, if he's not with someone, he always wants to be," Andie reminded us. "This will pass as soon as he links up with his next victim."

The twins laughed. "She's right," Paula said.

"Well, I sure hope so." I poured my chocolate milk into a glass.

"So ... what's everyone think about the new Marty Leigh book?" I asked.

Andie snorted. "*Everybody's* not reading that book!"

I grinned. "You're right, and what a mistake. You're totally missing out."

Kayla nodded. "I love how she wraps everything up in the end. It's really amazingly satisfying and wonderful."

"Don't tell me what happens," I said, dying to know, but eager to read it for myself.

Paula fluffed her hair, frowning. "I have a feeling I know exactly where you got your ideas about living with your dad."

"What do you mean?" I was playing dumb.

"You know—the joint custody thing in the book," Paula said. "It was Tricia's idea first, long before it was yours. I'm right, and I know it."

I thought back to last Saturday at the bookstore. I'd read the back of the book. Paula was right, I had gotten the idea from the book!

I sighed dramatically. "Look at it this way— maybe it was meant to be. Maybe I was supposed to read *Tricia's Secret Journey* right now—at this stage of my life."

"Oh, please! Surely you aren't saying it was planned by God," Andie said. "I think you're stirring up trouble for your mom and dad. They've already been through a divorce; why do you have to start something stupid like this?"

"My wishes and desires are not stupid!"

Andie stared at me. "I hardly know you any-more, Holly-Heart. It's like you're altered some-how . . . had a personality change."

"Really? Is that what you think?" I stared back at her, then at the twins. "Do *all* of you think this?"

"Well, I wouldn't go so far as to agree with the personality change," Paula spoke up, "but I do think you should wait, give your mom a chance to have her baby and settle into a few changes at your house, then decide. It's the kind thing to do."

Kayla was nodding her approval. "I agree with Paula. Why not wait and see how things go after the baby comes?"

"Seems like a logical suggestion to me," Andie said.

I took a long drink of chocolate milk. "Sounds like none of you are on my side."

"What do you mean, sides?" Paula asked. "This has nothing to do with taking sides."

"Seems like it," I muttered into my glass.

"Well, why don't you come to youth group tonight? You missed last week," Paula said.

"Yeah, we'll save you a seat," Kayla offered. "Okay?"

I gave in to their suggestion, realizing once again that they really *did* care. No one was siding against me. Not really.

❤   ❤   ❤

There was a substitute in French class, and the teacher hadn't the slightest idea how to either speak or write the language, so she gave us free study time.

Gratefully, I used the fifty minutes to work on my novella. Perfect! I had decided to wait until the very end of the book to think of a fabulous title, but the more I wrote, the more I realized that a good title was essential to the entire structure of the story.

That's what I'll do tonight, I thought. *After youth service.*

I would create a sensational title. Titles, after all, caught book editors' attention first. I certainly didn't want to lose the opportunity to impress Jared's publisher uncle.

Speaking of Jared, he was waiting for me after French class. "Hey, I found out about the deadline for our manuscripts." He fell in step with me.

"Really? What's the cutoff date?"

"April thirtieth."

"That's good," I said. "Mom's new baby will have arrived." It was perfect timing. "I should have my story finished long before then."

If all goes well at home, I thought.

"So, how's it coming—the writing, I mean?" he asked.

"Really great. How 'bout yours?"

"Cool." He flashed a heart-stopping grin. "Thanks for asking."

"It was just a simple question," I told him. "Don't read anything into it."

"Aw, Holly, stop being so defensive."

"I think it's time for me to go." I turned to leave.

No sense hanging around. Jared was still trying out his moves. Driving me crazy.

"Wait, uh, Holly. Would it be okay if I walked you to your locker?"

I studied him. This guy never, I mean *never*, gave up!

"C'mon, it's no big deal," he assured me. "Just a friendly gesture."

"Oh, all right. Come on." He had to hurry to keep up—it didn't turn out to be the romantic hall stroll he might've anticipated. Basically, Jared ran behind me all the way to my locker. It was ridiculous what I was doing to him, but I had my reasons. No way was he going to get the wrong idea about me ... us.

After school, I had to go straight home. Uncle Jack had told me in no uncertain terms during breakfast that I was on restriction. I wasn't surprised. I'd dished out some pretty nasty stuff to Mom this morning, not to mention my lousy attitude.

Mentally, I abandoned the power struggle over the after-school phoning rule and hurried to the bus stop. The rule wasn't worth the fight. Besides, I had a hunch there might be some mail waiting for me, so I didn't mind going right home.

My hunch was correct. Sean's letter lay on top of the pile of mail on the corner desk in the kitchen. Mom had probably placed it there so I'd see it right away. Funny. She never held a grudge. Never!

Quickly, I opened the envelope and leaned on the

island in the middle of the kitchen, reading the letter.

> *Saturday, January 20th*
> *Dear Holly,*
>
> *I'm afraid I have some bad news. Remember the group of middle schoolers I told you about—Power House? Well, several problems have come up with some of the younger kids—parental permission, finances, etc.—and it looks as though we aren't going to be coming to Dressel Hills to ski as planned.*
>
> *At the present time, the adult leaders are leaning toward going to San Diego for the weekend of February 16th, which is two days after your birthday.*
>
> *I'm very, very sorry about this turn of events, Holly. I had no idea our personal plans, yours and mine, would have to be altered like this.*
>
> *More than anything, I hope there will be many other opportunities to see each other.*

The words on the page faded, blurred in a flood of tears. *More than anything . . . other opportunities . . . not coming . . .*

I ran, sobbing, to my room.

"Something's wrong with Holly," I heard Carrie say as I closed my bedroom door. I wanted to lock it—shut the whole world out. Crying my eyes out was all I could do.

Poor Goofey, helpless to know how to comfort me, meowed out of concern and pushed his furry back up against me as I lay on the bed.

Minutes later, someone tapped on my door. "Holly?" It was Mom. "Is there anything I can do?"

I couldn't speak for the tears.

"Holly-Heart?"

This was one time—one of the very few times in my life—I desperately needed to be left alone. Ordinarily, when I was sad or depressed, I wanted someone to pursue me, help me through my pain even if I insisted I didn't. I was weird that way.

At this moment, however, I needed time to cry. Time to feel sorry for myself. Sean wasn't coming after all. Our plans, all of them, had melted away with this letter.

No one else ... *no one* could possibly understand what I was feeling. Any coaxing or offering of sympathy would be useless.

"Holly?" Mom called again.

"I can't talk now," I managed to say, hoping with all my heart she'd believe me and leave me alone.

"Okay, honey," she replied, "but I'm just down the hall if you need me."

Need me. Of course, I needed her. Maybe not at this instant, but later, if I ever got over this horrible disappointment. Mom was my mainstay, my rock-solid support in life—the one I'd always counted on, the only one who'd never really let me down.

But now, the way things were between us ... how could I possibly expect kind words from her after the heart-wrenching things I'd said this morning?

Holding the letter, I reread Sean's words. He wouldn't be coming for my fifteenth birthday. That meant there'd be no snow party with the Dressel Hills youth group. No first date with the one and only Sean Hamilton.

So much for bragging and blabbing about my California boyfriend! If only I'd kept my big mouth shut.

FIFTEEN

For the second week in a row, I couldn't bring myself to attend youth service. Andie and the Miller twins might think I'd deceived them by saying I was coming. I hoped not, because I'd fully intended to go when we discussed it at lunch.

But now . . . with my eyes swollen and my cheeks red from crying, well, it was totally pointless.

I stayed home and worked on my book title. *Nothing but the Heart* was one of my stronger title options. I knew it might not be the one I would end up with, but as a working title it spurred me on.

Miraculously, with Stan out of the house, and the rest of the kids at church clubs and things, I was able to write two more good chapters. I surprised myself. Usually, when I was in a gray mood like tonight, nothing, absolutely nothing, flowed when it came to writing. Sometimes, though, my writing was therapy. Tonight, it was just that—keeping my mind off the big disappointment.

When I went to the kitchen for some pop, Uncle Jack and I avoided each other—I being the only kid in the house for a few hours this evening. Mom didn't dodge me but seemed a little distant. Maybe she was hurt. Knowing Mom, she would survive. She always did.

As for me, things were piling up emotionally like the steady snowfall outside. First the baby news, then Sean's letter. What next?

My shoulders drooped as I headed back upstairs to edit my chapters.

Less than five minutes later Mom was at my door, knocking gently, almost hesitantly. "Your stepdad and I would like to see you for a minute." She stated it so formally, I wondered if there was going to be additional discipline heaped upon me for the way I'd behaved this morning. Maybe going without phone calls and having to come straight home from school today wasn't enough for my stepdad.

I dropped everything and left my room.

When I arrived, Uncle Jack was sitting at the dining-room table having another round of frozen yogurt pie. Mom pulled out a chair next to him, and I, wanting a cushion of space between myself and the powers-that-be, sat at the far end of the table.

Uncle Jack glanced at Mom before he began.

"Your father called here this afternoon, Holly ... spoke to your mother briefly."

I felt my throat constrict, go instantly dry.

"Your father's talking lawyers, court hearings, the works." He studied me with serious eyes. "You've created quite a stir in the family."

I was secretly pleased. Daddy was coming through for me after all these years!

Mom started to sniffle, reaching into her pocket for a tissue. I hoped she wouldn't cut loose and really start boo-hooing. But, at this advanced stage of her pregnancy, who was to know.

"As you can see," Uncle Jack continued, "your mother is taking every bit of this very hard, kiddo." He let his fork hang off the edge of his plate. "As for myself, I'd like to see this difficulty worked out for the best of everyone concerned."

"What about my best interests?" I blurted. "Isn't that what the judge will look at?"

Mom sighed, folding her hands on the table. "We're hoping it won't go that far. We'd like to be able to work things out with you."

"Me?" I coughed. "I'm the one feeling pushed out. You need my room for your nursery; I need the chance to breathe again. Daddy has the space for me to do that."

"We're in shock," Mom said through a veil of tears. "How can we ... I ... let you go? You're my first child, Holly-Heart. I love you so ..." Her voice trailed off, intermingled with tears.

"What's so wrong with splitting my time

between Colorado and California?" I wailed, having difficulty remaining calm.

"What's wrong with it is your attitude." Uncle Jack was getting up now. He began to walk back and forth, rubbing his hands together like he was stirring up his thoughts. "You aren't working with us—you're fighting us. Fighting everything we're trying to do for you."

"How can you say that?" I shot back.

"Think about it," he said softly.

I drew a deep breath. "Oh, I know, this must be about that stupid rule—that after-school phoning rule. You think I should just comply with it, even though I'm older now. Lots older than when Mom first created it. I never complained about it all those years before."

Uncle Jack stood behind Mom's chair, rubbing her shoulders gently as she cried. "I don't think we're getting anywhere with this." He looked over at me, concern in his eyes. "I want you to promise me one thing, Holly, and your father is now in agreement with this, too."

What was he going to say?

"We—all of us—want you to spend time praying about the joint custody decision. We'll be praying, too."

Mom was literally sobbing. Uncle Jack leaned down and whispered, "I think it would be best if you'd rest now, honey." He kissed her on the top of her head. "We surely don't want anything to happen. Not now."

Mom got up with Uncle Jack's help, leaving the dining room with sobs. I was outraged. Uncle Jack had just implied that I might be causing problems for Mom—for her pregnancy! How could he say that?

I would never do anything to cause Mom to lose . . . to lose the baby, I thought. *Never!*

The anger pounded in me. I stared at the man who was my uncle and stepdad rolled up in one. It was all I could do to control myself. Holding in my frustration only brought indignant tears, and I let them fall unchecked.

"You think I've planned this—set all this up—to make Mom have trouble with her pregnancy?" I said, my words pouring out with a vengeance. "Is that what you think?"

He looked at me with bewildered eyes, standing there silently.

"You know me better than that!" I shouted. And with that, I flew out of the room and up the stairs.

SIXTEEN

The next week was a blur of unhappiness. At least, for me. Everyone else in the house seemed to be involved in some baby activity or another.

There remained an unspoken aura of tension between Uncle Jack and me. Mom kept to herself, however. I was beginning to wonder if she'd ever get used to the situation, the fact that I wanted to split my time between her and Daddy. Usually, Mom took things in her stride. But when it came to heart matters such as these, I guess Mom simply couldn't pull herself out of the doldrums.

I didn't get around to calling the attorney's office back. The way I saw it, if Daddy was actually willing to consider the possibility, I'd rather use his private family attorney than have the state appoint one for me here. As for proceeding with the legal side of things, I wasn't sure what I was waiting for. Maybe the fact that everyone had insisted I pray about it. Maybe that was what was holding me back.

I hadn't obeyed them. All week, I avoided the prayer issue, even neglected my personal devotions. Deep within myself, I recognized my problem. I was stubborn and unwilling to let God work in me. I wanted things my way or not at all. Yet, I was too headstrong to change my course.

Carrie was the one who got me charged up about things again. I was cleaning my room after school when she knocked on my door.

"Hi," she said, wide-eyed, with her hair in a long ponytail high on her head. The way I used to wear mine. "I heard you want outta here."

"Oh, really?" Mom had finally gotten around to informing the rest of the family, it seemed. I closed the door behind her, allowing her into my private domain.

"You know what I think? I think it stinks," she said, and before I could comment, she began to cry.

"Carrie, what's wrong?" I went over to where she stood in front of my dresser, burying her head in her hands. Stunned, I wrapped my arms around her. "It's okay, you don't have to cry."

But cry, she did. Not just a little, either. Heartbreaking sobs poured from her. "Don't leave, Holly ... please, don't go away ..."

I felt my own eyes watering, that's how incredibly crushed Carrie sounded. Waiting for her to calm down, I finally spoke. "I hope you don't think I want to go away because of you." The thought had occurred to me while she was bawling. I didn't want Carrie to think just because she was turning into a snooty little so-and-so that I was abandoning her.

"Mom said you needed some space—to get away from here for a while," she blubbered. "I don't see what's so bad about living here."

I tried to explain. "It's not just the space. It's other things, too."

She looked up at me suddenly, her tearful eyes demanding answers. "Like what other things? What could possibly be so awful about living here?"

"I didn't say it was awful."

"You know how much Mom . . . how much I love you."

"And I love you, too." I hugged her.

"But not Mom, is that it?"

"Of course not, silly. That's not it at all." I was groping for words. Everything I wanted to say to her sounded so trite inside my head.

"Then is it about the baby?" she asked, wiping her eyes.

I waited a few seconds before responding. "The baby's a big problem for me, I guess you could say."

She didn't understand. I knew by the incredulous look on her face. "How can you say that?"

I shook my head. It was no use. "I can't explain it."

"You're jealous, then, that must be it."

I hated her for saying that. Everyone was saying it. Even Andie. "Why should I be jealous of an unborn baby, for Pete's sake?"

She stared at me, determination in her eyes. "It's written all over your face."

I chuckled. "You're sounding more like Mom every day."

"So that's it, huh? You have nothing to say for yourself."

At that moment, I wanted to escort her—no, I wanted to *throw* her out of my room. The haughty little brat! "I don't need a lecture from you." I went to the door and opened it wide.

"Someone should talk sense to you. You're making our mother sick, Holly. Why don't you think about someone else besides yourself, for a change?" In a huff, she bounced out of the room.

It was impossible to work on my novella that night. Algebra came first, of course, and later, I attempted to add another chapter to my novella. Nothing came. The words were scrambled up in my brain, so how could I expect to sort them out on paper?

Along about ten o'clock, I gave up and went to bed. My sleep was erratic and filled with weird dreams. Even Goofey was restless and finally left his cozy spot on my bed for the peaceful solitude of the window seat.

The next morning, I felt lousy when the shrill sound of the alarm awakened me. I stumbled into the bathroom and reached for the shower knobs, hoping the warm water would soothe my tired body and spirit.

While I let the water run against my back, I

thought of Kayla's questions about Stan—a mild relief from the real frustrations of my life. What could *I* do to reveal Kayla's ongoing crush to my brousin? Why were guys so dense anyway?

One thing led to another, and soon I was mulling over Jared Wilkins. Again. Why did it seem I never quite got the guy out of my head? I was as good as Sean's girl!

These days, I could honestly say I never thought about Jared in terms of a boyfriend. If what Amy-Liz had told me was true months ago—that she broke up with him because he couldn't stop talking about me—well, that was hard to believe, and even if that really was the reason, I had a hard time bringing myself to consider Jared as more than just a good friend. Funny thing, we *were* that—good friends. In fact probably closer friends, at least at the present time, than when he and I were going out. Amazing, but true.

What would Sean think if he knew I was thinking about Jared this way? What would my future husband, whoever he was, think if he knew how emotionally caught up I was over both Jared and Sean?

I couldn't determine how, or from what submerged brain cells the impulse came, but suddenly the disturbing notion was there—certainly uninvited, perfectly crazy.

Sean Hamilton wanted out—that's why he'd written the letter. Could it be true—was my impulse correct? Was his excuse about the Power

House group not being able to come to ski merely a convenient way for Sean to call it quits?

Briskly, I dried off, anxious to reread his letter. But by doing so, I only felt more rejected, reading things between the lines that may or may not have really been there. I was more frustrated than ever and fussed over my hair for no reason. It was easy to manage now that the spiral perm had relaxed. Except for the shorter length, I actually liked my hair. Sean had written that he liked it, too, upon receiving a recent photo from me. He'd gone on and on about how pretty I looked.

But you are pretty on the inside, too, which is far more important to me. He'd written that, and I'd believed him. But now? Now he wasn't coming and making no effort to reschedule another time. What did he expect me to think?

Mom didn't show up for breakfast, so us kids did our fending routine and managed just fine. Basically, Stan and I saw to it that everyone bowed their heads for prayer and ate a well-rounded breakfast before heading off to our separate schools.

I couldn't help thinking about the playpen or high chair soon to be making its appearance in the kitchen. Babies didn't stay little long. They grew up rapidly, threw applesauce and oatmeal all over the floor, and made big messes.

When breakfast and cleanup were over, I hurried to the bus stop, eager to see my school friends.

All of them—Jared included.

SEVENTEEN

Jared was almost enticing when he stopped by my locker before lunch. He wore a plaid flannel shirt that brought out the bright blue in his eyes, and for a change, I actually listened as he told two jokes, one right after the other.

"You're in rare form today," I commented as we walked toward the school cafeteria.

"Hey, I like what I'm hearing." He turned to look at me, laughing flirtatiously.

I refused to allow things to get out of hand between us. That's why I headed straight for the table where Andie, the Miller twins, and I usually sat at lunchtime. I had to be careful. It wouldn't be fair to soak up Jared's obvious interest just to divert my own thoughts and change my mood. I wouldn't use him that way.

"What's the latest about living in California?" Andie asked as she, Paula, and Kayla converged on us.

"I'm waiting to make my decision," I stated.

Paula smiled. "Waiting till after your mom has her baby?"

"Not that long," I replied, not telling her that I'd been told to spend time in prayer about my choice. I still hadn't.

"What's going to be the determining factor?" Kayla asked.

I glanced around at them— each of them—feeling suddenly overwhelmed with their presence. "Can we drop this for now?" I gave them a weak smile. "I have a lot to think about."

Jared was first to agree. "Yeah, let's give Holly some breathing room."

Andie caught my eye and gave her wordless warning. I knew she didn't want me going soft on Jared. I wouldn't disappoint her; she just didn't know it yet.

Jared brought up the subject of a Valentine ski party. "Pastor Rob's been talking a lot about it. What do you guys think?"

I held my breath as Andie jumped in on the conversation. She didn't know—no one knew—about Sean's letter or that he wasn't coming.

"Well, Holly's boyfriend is coming from California with a bunch of middle-school kids. What do you say we include them?" Andie said.

"Fine with me." Paula studied me with a question

mark in her eyes, probably wondering why I wasn't responding.

"That's cool," Jared said, but his expression gave him away. He didn't really think Sean's coming was cool at all.

"Good idea," Andie continued. "What do you think, Holly-Heart?" She looked right at me.

"Maybe next year," I said, deciding to level with them. "Sean and his youth group are going to San Diego instead."

Andie gasped. "No," she cried. "Oh, Holly." She reached over and grabbed my hand. "You must be totally devastated."

I forced a smile. "Not exactly."

"Yes, you are," she insisted. I knew it was all a show for Jared's sake—so he wouldn't go getting any romantic ideas about me.

"Really, it's okay." I pleaded with my eyes for her to drop the subject. But she kept it up. That is, until I picked up my tray and left the table.

I wasn't surprised; Jared got up, too, following close behind as I headed for the kitchen to return my tray. "Are you okay with this ... this cancellation?" he asked.

He's fishing, I thought.

"There'll be other times," I said.

Andie was headed our way, plowing through a group of students, frantically trying to get to me. I don't know why she didn't trust me. Didn't she know I wasn't going to fall for Jared's sweet talk just because Sean wasn't coming? I wasn't stupid!

"Oh, Holly," she called, displaying a desperate look. "Walk with me to my locker." She completely avoided Jared, who stood beside me. "Come on!"

"Excuse me," I called to Jared over my shoulder.

"See ya after school," I heard him say as we hurried down the hall.

"What do you think you're doing?" I demanded. "I can take care of myself."

Andie snorted. "Didn't look like it to me."

We were coming up on her locker. A group of upperclassmen were hanging around nearby. Three of them glanced at us as though we were slime. What else was new? This was high school, after all.

"Smile!" Andie called to them, only to receive the cold shoulder and some loud, disparaging howls of laughter. At times like these, I wished I were home-schooled.

Not Andie. She loved social challenges. "C'mon, you can force a smile for us lowly freshmen," she shot back.

"Andie," I whispered. "Cut it out." This time I was the one grabbing her arm and hauling her away to my locker.

"What are you doing?" she asked.

"Saving you from yourself." I kept going, dragging her along.

Reluctantly, she followed me to my locker. I made her hold my books while I searched in my purse for Sean's letter. "Here," I said, finding it. "Read this and tell me what you think." I pushed the letter into her face.

"I can't read it that close," she complained, piled up with my books.

I stepped back, still holding the letter as she began to scan it. "So ... what do you think?" I asked.

She shrugged. "About what? He's not coming, it's that simple."

"But ... do you think he's dumping me?"

Andie frowned and shook her head. "I don't get that from reading this, why?"

I sighed. "Once more—read it again."

She did. "Nope. It's not curtains for Sean Hamilton."

"You're absolutely positive?"

"What are you worried about?" she asked.

"Just a feeling I have."

"Well, your feeling's wrong." She handed back my books. "Didja write him back?"

"Not yet."

"You'll be getting another letter from him, you'll see."

Going on Andie's instincts, I felt okay about answering Sean's letter, which I did during French class. Most of the class was studying for a test scheduled for tomorrow. I figured I could review my dialogues that night. Easy.

Surprisingly, I felt better once the letter was written. Not because I'd written in a positive, upbeat manner, but because my best friend thought I was mistaken about why Sean wasn't coming. To tell the truth, thinking that she was right was one less burden to carry around. The mental and emotional load was still weighing me down. And now I had another burden to add: Mom's ultrasound results. Also scheduled for tomorrow.

Tomorrow, on the first day of February—the beginning of my birthday month—the doctor would probably be able to determine whether Mom's baby was a boy or a girl. On top of that, if the ultrasound pictures were clear, Uncle Jack was going to play a video of it for the family. Like he thought we were interested or something.

Personally, I couldn't imagine spending tomorrow evening viewing such a thing—an unborn baby floating around inside my mother's stomach. The very same baby who was upsetting my entire life!

EIGHTEEN

After school the next day, both Andie and Jared were waiting at my locker. Andie's scowl gave her away—she wasn't thrilled that he'd shown up again. She totally dominated the conversation, on purpose. In fact, there was no time for Jared to say what was on his mind before we had to leave to catch the bus.

"Okay if I call you?" Jared asked as the three of us headed down the hall.

"Of course," I said, smiling. "I'll look forward to it."

Andie nearly died on the spot but was polite enough not to make a rude remark. Jared said good-bye to both of us and hurried off in the opposite direction to the library.

"About Jared," Andie said as she and I waited at the bus stop. "You're leading him on."

"I'm being polite," I assured her. "There's nothing to worry about."

"Aw, c'mon, you know what'll happen."

"What? What can happen if I don't want to get back together with him?"

She was silent. But only for a few seconds. "So . . . are you really going to push this joint custody thing through?"

"Of course. It's the best thing in the world for me."

"For you? Since when does your family's life revolve around one person?" She'd launched off on one of her pet peeves. "Families are a community effort—they're forever, girl, and don't you forget it."

"I didn't say they weren't, but if I remember correctly, we've already had this conversation. If you don't mind, could we please drop it?" I'd had it with her know-it-all attitude.

"Well, excu-use me. If I can't talk sense to you, Holly, who can?"

I kept my mouth shut even though I knew she was baiting me. The atmosphere was heavy with conflict, ripe for a fight. Besides that, Andie's biggest hang-up lately was irrational worry over the future. In other words, what would happen to us—our friendship, our close bond—after high school, college, and beyond? The question had plagued both of us in recent months.

"So . . . aren't we talking now?" she asked.

"The bus is coming." That's all I could say without getting into a word war.

"Okay, fine. No more talk of California or joint custody," she volunteered. "I promise."

"What about Jared?"

She shook her head. "Do whatever you want about him."

"Really?" I said, elated. "Did I hear you correctly? You're actually giving me permission to live my life without constant editing from you?"

Andie ignored my snide ranting and boarded the bus.

Case closed. At last!

❤   ❤   ❤

I couldn't wait to get back to *Tricia's Secret Journey*, but first I worked through my French homework on the bus.

Back home, Carrie and Stephie had already claimed the dining-room table, spreading their homework every which way. Phil was using the kitchen bar for his space. Mark was outside playing in the snow, and Stan still wasn't home from school. As best as I could calculate, Stan had ten more minutes before he should be calling home. The after-school calling rule remained in force. Even for male sophomores.

Mom was resting quietly in her room, and Uncle Jack was still downtown at his consulting firm. No one else was upstairs. Fabulous—everyone in the house was occupied at the same time. I curled up beside Goofey and opened my book.

As always, Marty Leigh's writing pulled me into the familiar fiction world I loved. Tricia Joellyn had succeeded in getting the joint custody issue resolved and was now living six months out of the year with her dad and stepmom. However, she'd discovered a mystery while there.

Yes! The suspenseful part, at last, I thought.

I had actually begun to wonder why this book was classified as a mystery. But here it was, an incredibly suspenseful last third of the book. Tricia had uncovered a long-kept family secret—there was a twin sister she'd never known. The girls had been separated at birth. Somewhere out in the vast world, Tricia's twin lived with another set of parents—adoptive parents. A girl with Tricia's face. But where?

I was so engrossed in the plot, I never even heard my name being called. Stan had come home, evidently bringing someone with him, or so Carrie was saying as I opened my bedroom door to her. "I've been calling you, Holly."

"Uh, sorry." I marked my page with my finger, still absorbed with the book.

"Someone's downstairs to see you," she said. "One of your girlfriends."

Reluctantly, I searched for a bookmark and closed the book, wondering what girlfriend of mine would be coming home with Stan.

I heard Kayla Miller's bright, cheerful laughter. She'd managed to get Stan's attention, it seemed. Without my help. This was fascinating!

I headed downstairs, eager to see her. "Hi, Kayla," I greeted her as I came into the living room. "What's up?"

Kayla's eyes sparkled. "Stan's going to be my project partner."

Stan had already begun to unroll some wide sketching paper across the living-room floor. "We're making a time line for world history class," he informed me.

I grinned at Kayla. "Really?"

She nodded. "We chose the Middle Ages. It's due next week."

"Cool." I was dying to know who'd asked whom, but didn't want to embarrass Kayla.

It turned out that Stan drove Kayla home after supper. I observed the way the two of them interacted comfortably in front of Mom and Uncle Jack and the rest of the family at the table. They were a good match. Kayla had been right all along.

I was putting the last plate in the dishwasher when Jared called. "Hello?" I said, getting it on the first ring so there'd be no competition in the house.

"Hi," Jared said. "I wish we could've talked earlier. After school."

I laughed. "We're talking now."

"Guess you're right." He paused, as though he were getting up the nerve to ask me something. "Uh, Holly, I've been doing a lot of thinking— mostly praying, though."

Strange, hearing Jared Wilkins talk this way.

"I think God's telling me that you shouldn't continue pursuing the joint custody thing," he said.

"Telling *you?*" I chuckled. "Who is this talking, really?"

He didn't laugh. "I'm serious, Holly." He didn't go on and on trying to persuade me. His words were brief and to the point. This approach was refreshing after having put up with Andie's constant nagging on the subject. She never could just make her point and stop. Overkill.

I wanted to hear more. "You think God's telling you this . . . for me?"

"You sound surprised," he said. "I thought you'd be getting the same sort of spiritual direction."

"What do you mean?"

He didn't answer for a moment. "You are praying about this, aren't you?"

I was caught. What could I say? I felt humiliated. Here was Jared, praying about my future circumstances!

"Holly?"

I took a deep breath. "To be honest with you, I haven't prayed about joint custody. Not really."

"You're kidding," he said. "Something that life-altering, and you haven't—"

"This is *my* business," I interrupted.

"I can see that." He said it firmly, almost sternly. "Well, I guess I don't have anything more to say to you. Other than, I'm praying you'll do things God's way." Jared said good-bye and hung up.

I was baffled by his words. If I hadn't known better, I would've thought he'd conferred with Danny Myers, the most spiritual guy in our entire youth group. Had someone coached Jared on what to say just now?

Surely not. Yet what an amazing change, and Andie thought I was the one undergoing a temperament change. Whew, this was unbelievable!

I couldn't wait to tell someone. Anyone!

NINETEEN

The following evening, Uncle Jack was rounding everyone up. Time to watch Mom's baby swim around in her tummy. I couldn't believe I was actually going to sit through this event.

Mom settled down in her favorite spot in the family room downstairs—on the far end of the sectional. The arm was wide and comfortable there, and she propped several throw pillows behind her back.

Stan, Phil, Mark, Carrie, and Stephie sat cross-legged on the floor in front of the TV screen, eager for the show to begin. I, however, perched on the edge of the sectional at the opposite end from Mom and Uncle Jack. The way I figured, a noncommittal attitude was the best way to go on a night like this.

"Show us our new baby!" Carrie called out as Uncle Jack used the remote to rewind. Evidently, he'd already previewed the video. His enthusiastic smile gave him away.

Not a word had been said at supper about whether the baby was a boy or a girl. Top secret info. Maybe Uncle Jack, being the unorthodox kind of guy he was, really and truly wanted this to be a memorable moment for the family.

"We should have a meeting after the video, to name the baby," Mark said.

Uncle Jack looked Mom's way. "What do you say, honey? Good idea?"

She nodded, pushing a loose strand of hair out of her face. "I'm open for any and all suggestions. Within reason." She had to say that, of course, since we had several comedians in the family.

"You're on, Mark. Great idea," Uncle Jack said, to which Mark and Phil gave each other high fives.

Must be a boy, I thought. They probably already know ... Of course, someone to carry on the Patterson name. Not that Uncle Jack needed another son! But Mom—she'd probably be thrilled. She'd never given birth to a boy.

"Okay, kill the lights," Uncle Jack said, nestling back into the sectional next to Mom.

The video began.

Reluctantly, I watched as a shadowy, almost ethereal image projected itself on the screen. My eyes scanned the ultrasound picture. Then I saw it—the fetus, curled up in a snug position. Sucking its thumb.

Uncle Jack began to narrate as we watched. "Each of us grows from one tiny cell, smaller than a grain of sand, to a full-grown baby of about seven or eight pounds."

"How long is a baby when it's ready to be born?" Stephie asked in the darkness.

"Around twenty or twenty-one inches," Mom replied. "You and Holly were both a little over twenty-one inches at birth."

"Will *this* baby be that long?" Phil asked.

Who cared about lengths and pounds. What was this kid, anyway—male or female? Wasn't that what this viewing session was all about?

Uncle Jack kept talking about the way babies grow and prepare for birth. I knew all this stuff. Eventually, though, I found myself paying closer attention, looking for evidence to indicate that Mom's baby might be a boy.

Stephie was the least shy one in the bunch. "I can't tell anything," she said. "How do we know if the baby's a boy or girl?" There were several snickers in the darkness.

Uncle Jack explained about human anatomy, careful not to embarrass any of us as he got up and went to the TV screen. He was cool that way. I mean, I didn't know many fathers—er, uncles-turned-step-dads—who could handle a subject so delicately. Anyway, Stephie seemed satisfied.

Uncle Jack came back and sat down, watching from his cozy spot with Mom. Then I heard him quote the verses from Psalm 139. The ones that always made me shiver when I realized how much God had loved me, even before I was ever born.

"'For you created my inmost being; you knit me together in my mother's womb. I praise you because I am fearfully and wonderfully made . . .'"

Wonderfully made . . . this little child . . .

"The baby's a girl," I blurted, without thinking.

"Holly's right," Uncle Jack said. "We're going to have another little girl."

I held my breath, watching. My soon-to-be little sister—tiny hands and feet, fingers and toes—perfectly formed. The more I watched, the more I had to fight back the tears. What a horrible big sister I had been, treating this precious God-ordained life with disdain. With resentment.

In the dim light of the video, I stole a glance at Mom and Uncle Jack. Happy newlyweds, anticipating the birth of their firstborn child, together. What heartbreaking sadness each of them had endured. Lonely, grievous times. Now they had each other. And all of us.

Eight isn't enough, I thought. Not when you have plenty of love to go around. Mom and Uncle Jack certainly did. That was, and had been, clear all along. I'd been too stubborn, too caught up in my selfish plans, to see the truth.

Jared was right. God's way was always best. Always.

I studied my siblings—the tops of their heads silhouetted against the bright screen ahead—as they sat, watching, spellbound on the floor. We were a family, all eight of us. In April this little child growing safely inside of Mom would make us nine.

I could hardly contain myself. "We should name her April," I said as the video ended. "It's the perfect name."

I caught a glimpse of Mom's smile as Stan turned on the lights. "April's a lovely name," she said. "In fact, I wrote it down just yesterday as a possibility."

Our baby-naming meeting had officially begun. Carrie and Stephie had several ideas, but in the end the name April stuck. Phil and Mark tried to get Mom to consider names like Jo or Dale for the baby's middle name, but those got vetoed quickly. In the end, all of us—all eight of us—agreed that April Michelle went very well with Patterson.

April Michelle. Our new little family member was greatly loved. Already!

"Are there any other things we should talk about?" asked Uncle Jack, looking at me.

I nodded. And for the first time, I asked the question that had been burning in me for days. "I've been wondering why Mom waited so long to tell us about the new baby."

Mom leaned forward. "We wanted to be absolutely sure everything was going well," she began. "You see, back in October, I almost lost our baby."

I gasped.

Uncle Jack continued. "Do you remember all those nights of frozen pizzas when Mom stayed upstairs in bed?"

I remembered all right. I'd worried that Mom had the flu or something. But this? Almost losing Baby April. The thought brought tears to my eyes.

"That's why we waited," Mom assured me. "Waited until we knew for sure."

Stephie and Carrie asked a few more questions. "Are we having a baby shower?" Carrie asked.

"Probably not," Mom said, smiling. "You usually only get a shower for the first baby."

"When are we going shopping for baby furniture?" asked Stephie.

Mom laughed, reaching for the catalog on the coffee table. "We ordered everything almost two weeks ago. Have a look."

Stephie and Carrie scooted over to inspect the yellow baby crib, dresser, and changing table to match. "Oh, you played it safe," Carrie observed. "This was before you knew we were having a sister."

"That's right," Mom said. "We didn't want to have something too fussy or too tailored."

The next question was on the tip of my tongue— where were they going to put the furniture?—but Uncle Jack announced that we were all going out for ice cream. "Your mother's been craving some peppermint ice cream all day."

I giggled. "What about some peppermint tea and honey?"

"Cravings have a way of changing during pregnancy," Mom said, laughing as Uncle Jack winked at her.

I could hardly wait for some time alone with the two of them. There was so much I needed to say. *I'm sorry* was only the half of it!

TWENTY

After school the next day, I worked on the last two chapters of my novella. It was amazing what could be accomplished in a short time, especially when the writer wasn't caught up in stressful life-battles. Feeling full of confidence, I knew I would finish *Nothing but the Heart* in plenty of time to submit it.

Before going to bed, I wrote in my journal. Time to get caught up with the private record of my life.

Friday, February 2nd: It didn't take long for me to get things out in the open with Mom and Uncle Jack last night. After that incredible ultrasound video, well, things totally changed for me—the way I view things around here, at least.

First off, I apologized for the crummy way I'd treated Mom and Uncle Jack. I even offered to share my bedroom with Baby April whenever they were ready to set up the crib.

Of course, I have no idea how all that'll work out, but I figure by the time I graduate from high school and head off to college (about three-and-a-half years from now), my baby sister will already be a toddler. How hard could it possibly be sharing my beautiful, spacious room with someone named April Michelle?

Oh . . . the joint custody issue is pretty much solved by the fact that I no longer sense a conspiracy between Mom and Uncle Jack. There had been one reason, and only one reason, why Mom hadn't told her special secret. Fear of miscarriage. Knowing what I know now, her decision makes perfect sense. I plan to call Daddy tomorrow and fill him in on my decision. After talking to the Lord, I know what I'm supposed to do.

Last night, at the end of our talk, Uncle Jack said something really fabulous. Some cool quote from a philosopher guy named Kierkegaard. I really like it, especially in terms of my recent blunder. I hope I never forget it. Here it is: "Life can only be understood backwards; but it must be lived forward."

Everything, right down to the anger and belligerence that prompted me to call an attorney's office, and to get Daddy all upset, EVERYTHING is clear to me now. I fully understand my life, this segment of it, at least.

Jared and I had a long talk today at lunch. We ate by ourselves until Andie and the Miller twins showed up and tried to rescue me. They were mistaken, of course; I didn't need rescuing at all. Jared and I are friends again. Good friends and nothing more. Someone else holds a special

place in my heart. Someone who's never given me any rea-
son to distrust him. Someone who's seeking God for guid-
ance about his own personal future. And for mine.

I doubt whether Jared heard God telling him I should
drop the joint custody issue. But his comments got me
thinking more about prayer, and I'm happy to say that
I'm keeping the heavenly lines of communication open
again. I missed talking to my number-one BEST friend.

I put my pen down and closed my journal.
Reaching for my Bible, I turned to Psalm 139—the
Scripture Uncle Jack had recited to us while we
watched our baby sister float inside Mom's stomach. "For you created my inmost being; you knit
me together in my mother's womb."

This verse was awesome. The more I thought
about it, the more I realized something powerful.
This same Creator-God who knew me and made me
also knew my future. He knew what would happen
between Sean Hamilton and me. He knew whether
or not I'd have a first real date on or after my fifteenth birthday. He also knew if or whom I'd marry,
if I'd have children—all that kind of important stuff.

I'd needed a lesson in trust. To learn to trust
God's plans for my life. The way Mom had entrust-
ed her unborn child to the care of the heavenly
Father.

"Thank you, Lord," I prayed, "for loving this
family of eight enough to give us a bonus baby.
And thanks for helping me accept the perfect plan
you have for me. Amen."

♥ About the Author ♥

Beverly Lewis has always loved the verses in Psalm 139 describing the love of our Creator-God. "It's comforting to know that the same God who formed us in our mother's womb, who knows the amount of individual hairs we're washing, styling, and spraying each day, also sees the fears and concerns of our lives," she says. "God sees and understands!"

Because of the increased volume of fan mail, Beverly requests that you please include a self-addressed envelope with a stamp on it when you write. Thanks!

Beverly Lewis
Author Relations
Zondervan Publishing House
Grand Rapids, MI 49530

Don't Miss the Other Holly's

HOLLY'S FIRST LOVE
Book #1 0-310-38051-0
The new boy at school threatens to destroy
Holly's relationship with her best friend, Andie.
Holly has a secret plan, but when it backfires, she
learns the meaning of friendship and the miracle
of forgiveness.

SECRET SUMMER DREAMS
Book #2 0-310-38061-8
Holly wants to visit her father in California for the summer, but the idea doesn't
make either her best friend, Andie, or her mother very happy. Holly gets some advice
from Danny, who seems to have more than just a big brotherly concern. Will Holly
make it to California?

SEALED WITH A KISS
Book #3 0-310-38071-5
When Holly and Andie have a pen-pal contest, Holly gets a male pen pal who is in
college. To impress him, she lies about her age. He then writes that he is coming to
Dressel Hills for a visit. What should Holly do?

THE TROUBLE WITH WEDDINGS
Book #4 0-310-38081-2
Holly's mother is getting married, and Holly is determined to make it a memorable
wedding—against her mother's wishes. Meanwhile, Holly tests her former "first love"
to see if he's really changed.

CALIFORNIA CHRISTMAS
Book #5 0-310-43321-5
Holly and her sister receive a surprise Christmas invitation to visit their father in
California. While there, Holly meets a California surfer, Sean, and her faithfulness to
her boyfriend back home is tested.

SECOND-BEST FRIEND
Book #6 0-310-43331-2
When Holly's best friend, Andie, invites her Austrian pen pal to Dressel Hills, jeal-
ousy erupts as Christiana moves in on Holly's friendship with Andie.

GOOD-BYE, DRESSEL HILLS
Book #7 0-310-44410-1
Holly is moving away from Dressel Hills, and she has just two weeks to say good-bye
to all her friends. She wonders whether to continue a "long-distance" relationship with
Jared, or to break it off now. To top it off, the surfer she met in California wants to
come visit. What should Holly do?

Heart Books in the Series!

STRAIGHT-A TEACHER
Book #8 0-310-46111-1

Holly develops a crush on the new teacher at school, and he soon becomes the focus of her attention. Her best friend, Andie, wonders if Holly's lead in the spring musical is a result of the handsome teacher playing favorites.

THE "NO-GUYS" PACT
Book #9 0-310-20193-4

It's the summer after eighth grade, and Holly's youth group goes to church camp. A couple of the girls have just had fights with their boyfriends, and all the girls make a pact to ignore the boys for the week of camp. Find out what happens when a war of the sexes results! Includes recipes, a pen-pal club, and tips from Holly.

LITTLE WHITE LIES
Book #10 0-310-20194-2

Holly and Andie are in California visiting Holly's dad when Andie falls for an eighteen-year-old surfer. Holly must choose between covering for her friend and telling the truth. Includes an honesty quiz, a pen-pal club, and tips from Holly.

FRESHMAN FRENZY
Book #11 0-310-20842-4

Holly and Andie are in high school, and suddenly Andie is the popular one. How will Holly find her place in high school—and keep her friendship with Andie?

MYSTERY LETTERS
Book #12 0-310-20843-2

When Holly takes on the role of advice columnist for her high school newspaper, a mysterious letter writer begins asking her personal questions. Who is writing the weird letters—and why?

EIGHT IS ENOUGH
Book #13 0-310-20844-0

Holly's mother is expecting a baby! But Holly thinks eight is a big enough family—and threatens to go live with with her father in California.

IT'S A GIRL THING
Book #14 0-310-20845-9

Holly's world falls apart when her choir competition in Washington, D.C. conflicts with the birth of her new sibling. Can she go to Washington, D.C., or should she stay home and help with the baby?

We want to hear from you. Please send your comments about
this book to us in care of the address below. Thank you.

ZondervanPublishingHouse
Grand Rapids, Michigan 49530
http://www.zondervan.com